HOLD DOWN SERIES
PART 1

Hold

Him

Down

SHEEM'A

HOLD HIM DOWN

Copyright © 2015 **Tushima Warr**

Printed in the United States of America

ISBN-13:978-0692469637
ISBN-10:069246963X

Printed by Createspace 2015
Published by BlaqRayn Publishing Plus 2015

PROLOGUE

As I look in the rear view mirror and see the flashing lights, I say to myself what the fuck! They just flew right pass me. I take a deep breathe and continue on to my destination. I'm looking sexy, thinking big things and my outcome is to be richer. Thinking to myself, *I do not want to have to kill Marv but I will since he's so deep in the game now... His head so blown up, can't nobody tell him shit...*

As I pull up to the gate, the security sees it's me and lets me in. As I enter the house, the Butler says "they are in the meeting room..."

I walk pass a full-length mirror, checking myself out, DAMN I'M FINE AND LOOKING FABULOUS. I wearing red bottoms Christian Louboutin high waist shorts with a one-shoulder shirt, body glistening, my favorite lip-gloss by SHEEM'A called Flawlezz, and hair laid by my cuzzo Shika. I smell damn good. Shit I had to take a double look and tell myself.. *self u is fine as hell*.

I buzz to be ushered into the office. I take a deep breathe and enter. As I walk in, they all stand, looking as if they've been waiting on me. I say "ok lets get down to it" as if I am the boss. All they know is I'm the Bottom Bitch... I held it down for a real nigga caught slipping. *I have taken over and they don't even know it.* I am willing to kill the connect and take anybody out who stood in our way of getting out the game.

"So here's the deal... this last hundred mil is to be washed and we out! All of us should be set for life. He says he wants out but he wants everyone happy. What's y'all take on this?"

One of the lower generals had to state the obvious.

"The Hustlers ain't gone be too happy about this."

"You let me and Marv deal with the rest of them asses... they have no choice. They can always find another supplier. Keo, you good?"

Keo really didn't give much of a damn what happened as long as he got paid.

"Yeah.. I'm straight."

"Paul you good?" Paul, on the other hand, might pose a problem...if not now...sometime in the future. If he still had one.

"Yeah that's cool."

"After this, we can all sit back and take a trip." I gave them asses a side grin.

"Call me when it's done. I will pick up our share and y'all keep yours. Bottom Bitch out."

I got my keys and walk out that bitch as if I owned the place. I could see in their faces they were not happy. They were all money hungry and wanted to continue forever. I believe in the old adage "get in and get out" no need for being greedy. It had the uneasy feeling I'd probably have to take them out all at once. *Praying I don't but I will if they push me to it...*

HHD 1

SYMONE

My god baby and I are in the park, playing on the slide, having a great time. I love her as if she is my own. I call her "mini me," but her name is Janae. Oh yeah and I'm Symone, or Sy for short. Now that we're both tired and I've worn her out, I took her to grab something to eat before dropping her off home. After all this, I need a hot bubble bath. It's "ladies' night" and we're going to see the Bulls play, and anyone that knows me know that I am a SUPER fanatic fan. Oh yeah I'm TOO geeked! I love me some Noah, Rose, Deng, Boozer, Robinson and Gibson. Sheeeiiit....I love the whole damn squad!
As soon as I lay across my bed to relax, my phone rang.

"Hey baby," Kim said when I answered. He's always texting and calling me, and normally I blow him off but I decided to answer this time.

"What up K?" I responded.

"Why you don't never answer my calls or text?" he whined.

I rolled my eyes and smiled.

"Because I'm always busy."

"Sy ain't nobody THAT busy," he argued.

"K, between work, friends, my god kids, I barely have time for ME."

I could tell he was smiling when he said, "See what you need is a man."

I was blushing hard as hell.

"Yeah I do but I haven't got time for that either."

"I'll help you make time," he confidently offered.

I quickly argued, "I don't know you like that K."

But he was equally as quick with his responses.

"Well then let's GET to know each other. How about tonight?"

Sigh...sadly I had to crush his little dreams once again.

"Sorry....got plans."

He was very persistent and flattering though; he made me blush even harder when he suggested,

"What about tomorrow?"

I finally gave in. "Ok. I'm free for lunch."

He was absolutely geeked.

"Ok I'll take that!" he exclaimed, and he already had the place in mind.

"Meet me at Table 52 on West Elm at 11:00."

"Ok sounds great. I'll see you then." We said our goodbyes and hung up.

I checked the time and it was already 5:00. I turned on some music, laid out my clothes and quickly jumped in the shower. Hopefully I'll be on time this time because I'm ALWAYS the "late one."

Right when I was about to put my big toe in the tub, here Kesh go blowing me up. Shit!

"Hello Kesh I'm getting dressed now and no I'm not going to be late," I blurted into the phone.

Kesh, with her smart mouth ass, calmly and politely said,

"Bitch you lying. You not even dressed yet."

I couldn't even argue with her, so I negotiated with her.

"Give me 20 minutes; I WILL be ready. And the door is open so just come on up." I hung and up before she could say another word.

I quickly press play on my iPod and the sounds of R. Kelly's TP2 album filled the room. This my shit right here! I jumped in the shower and slathered my body in my favorite Caress body wash. Damn this smells so good!

I grabbed my robe and checked out my hair ---- yup....still amazing, thanks to my cousin. She KEEPS me on point. I oiled myself up with natural cocoa butter and marveled over my body. I absolutely love this 6'0, 200 lbs, 38D frame of mine, and my mocha-cocoa color skin and light brown eyes are the cherry on top.

I threw on my D Rose jersey with some Levis, along with my red and black Jordan's number 6's. I spritzed on some of my favorite Nicki Minaj Pink Friday perfume and slid on my Rolex and a bracelet.

Suddenly I heard Kesh's voice bellowing from downstairs, "Sy is you ready yet?"

I smirked and smugly replied,

"Yes, girl I'm dressed like I said I would be. AND with 2 minutes to spare thank you very much!"

She can never just go with the flow; she always got a snappy come back.

"Girl you know you Miss Prissy; taking all damn day to get dress."

I just hit her with the same line as always, "Shut up heffa. Let's go; I need a drink."

Lisa was waiting for us in my living room. Before we walked out the door, I told them about my lunch plans.

"Umm ladies. Why I got a lunch date tomorrow?"

"With who?" Kesh blurted out. I knew I had to refresh their memory, so I reminded them.

"You remember the guy I met like 3 months ago named Kim?"

Lisa remembered him right away.

"Oh yeah...dude with the girl name." She and Kesh both burst out laughing. I just looked at them and shook my head.

"Damn that's funny to you huh? You just laughing hard as hell. Yeah him. He wants to meet at Table 52."

Kesh was shocked when I said where he wanted to do lunch.

"Really? They kind of high, but at least he got taste I see. Hope you don't be late like always."

"Shut up heffa," I laughed.

I knew they wanted a drink and I think they see me as their personal bartender. So I fixed us all a drink before we left the house.

"Are y'all ready to see the Bulls whoop on the Pacers?" I chided. "I know you two are just going for the men, but I'm actually going for the game."

go Miss-Always-Got-A-Comment Kesh.

"Yeah, yeah yeah….we know; you say it at every game."

I handed them their drinks.

"Here you go: Ciroc and pineapple orange juice. It's called a Pineapple Delight. Trademarked already."

"Do you hear her?" Kesh nudged Lisa. "Talking bout 'trademarked already.' This bitch is definitely all about her business."

I winked at them and said, "You know how I do."

Kesh burst out laughing.

"Bitch all this money you got? You need to sit down, find yourself a man and have some kids."

'I got TWO kids," I reminded her, "yours and Lisa's. That's all I need. Now drink up and let's go. Who's driving?" They never wanna drive out west so I wasn't surprised when Lisa said, "Sy you are cuz we need to drink and we like your car."

As we headed to the United Center, my girls and I were talking mad shit and swallowing spit. We're super funny when we get together. I took another quick look at them and said,

"Damn! Y'all heffas dressed like we going to the club."

Kesh laughed.

"Sy we MUST be cute at ALL times. You never know who we might meet."

She made it seem like I was a bum so I had to check her right quick.

"Well I'm comfortable AND cute."

"Yeah....you're single too," Lisa retorted.

I don't know what made her that; she sounded just like Kim.

"So NOT true, I'm just very busy," I defended myself.

"Ain't nobody EVER too busy for some DICK," Kesh laughed, high-fiving Lisa.

"At least I got toys til I DO find me a man, boo!" I spat. "Where y'all man at?"

"Hell, hopefully at this game," Kesh snickered.

Once we got inside the arena, I made a beeline for the concession stand and placed my order.

"I want some nachos, some Skittles and a Pepsi please. Do either of you want something?" I asked, glancing over my shoulder at them.

Lisa the snack queen, says, "Yeah just give us the same."

"Excuse me sir, make that times three. They want to be like me."

Lisa and Kesh both yell out, "No we just like the same snacks."

"Whatever," I said. "Let's go….my boys bout to start playing."

"Damn this game good! D Rose on his shit tonight! And my boo Noah doing his thang too!"

I may as well had been talking to my damn self because these heffa's wasn't paying NO attention to the game. Instead they were sitting up in here with their faces all in their phones, taking selfies and shit.

"I sure am glad it's half time 'cause I sure got to pee," Kesh said. She grabbed Lisa by the arm.

"Girl let's go. You see them fine guys in the row ahead of us? They been peeping us the whole game. Watch this….hey fellas!"

They all turned around: two of them were quite handsome, but the other one was fine ass all hell, like Tyrese. Damnnn....is all I could think. I got wet instantly. I pointed to Lisa and Kesh to let them know they were the ones who spoke.

"So who single?" Kesh asked and they all piped up, "I am!"

I laughed and said, "I bet they all lying."

"Let me get one thing clear," Kesh explained.

"I don't do crazy-ass exes and I damn sure do NOT do baby momma drama."

Two of them turn back around real quick. I smiled and said, "Well, at least they honest."

'Tyrese look-alike' said, "So do you have a man/stalker?"

Kesh frowned her up face at him.

"Hell no! Who does that? Not a real man."

He made her smile with his snappy comeback.

"Well...at least not a man who can't move on."

'Tyrese' stunned her smart-ass speechless, so I butt in right quick to save her.

"Very, very true."

He knew he had her choked up, so he chuckled a little and said, "Let's grab some beer ladies."

He walked up to the concession stand and placed the order. "Six beers please." Everyone offered to pay. Damn check them out.

I said, "Kesh and Lisa they trying to impress y'all. I'm driving so make mine a lemonade please."

We all chit-chatted for about five minutes more and quickly made our way back to our seats. I guess Kesh forgot she had to pee.

Of course, the Bulls won and I was beyond geeked.

"Let's go ladies. Applebee's is calling my name."

Mr. Tyrese asked if we wanted to go. I crushed his little world when I said, "ummm…what is your name again?" even though I remembered it was Sam.

He smiled and said, "It's Sam."

I said, "Well SAM, my girl Kesh is definitely digging you, so even though Applebee's is not my fave spot, we can come hang for a little while."

Well, that "little while" turned into a few hours. We all had such a great time. Those fellas are absolutely hilarious. We ate, talked, laughed and cracked a TON of jokes. Sam was really digging

Kesh and she was sho nuff feeling him too. Lisa was ok, but I knew she'd probably much rather be with a woman than a man. So she was cool just shootin' the shit. When the evening was over, we all exchanged numbers and promised to make plans to get up again real soon.

I was so damn tired when we got back to my house, I fell asleep in my clothes, straight across my bed. Kesh and Lisa took up residence in each of the guest bedrooms for the night.

****

When I got up the next morning, I hit the intercom to their rooms.

"Come eat breakfast you freaky heffas."

I'd prepared us a meal of turkey bacon, eggs, grits, and toast, and poured us each a nice, tall glass of OJ.

"Here y'all go. I have to run to the boutiques and then the shop. I'll tell them y'all won't be in today. Selena will clean up; just put the dishes in the sink. I'll be back around 9:00. If you guys leave, please be sure you lockup."

Lisa, still half-sleep, groggily mumbled, "Honey, I'mma be right here. Soon as I finish eating, I'm going right back and lay down."

Kesh chimed right behind her.

"Shit me too. I am beyond tired and I think I got a hangover. I need some BC powder."

"It's in the medicine cabinet in the guest bathroom," I told her. "Towels are in there also. Would you like to know where y'all clothes at too? I mean, damn do y'all live here?"

They both laughed and said,

"Uh...yes we do. Do you want us to move out?"

I laughed with them and said, "Please...y'all hoes ain't bothering me."

****

I own two boutiques: *Phat K'outure* and *Elegance and Beyond*, as well as a hair salon called *Alice Styles*, after my grandma. I quickly ran by all three and grabbed receipts and cash for the bank drop. I spoke to my cuz, Shika, at the salon and told her I would be in to see her the following day for a new hairdo; I made my bank deposit and dashed back home to get dressed for my lunch date with Kim.

I was determined not to be late, so I took a quick shower, did my routine and threw on a nice maxi sundress with some wedge heels and changed my purse. Kesh and Lisa were sprawled out on the couch in the living room, watching TV, half-asleep.

"Bye chicks," I said as I headed out the door. "I'll call later to let you two know how it goes." I made it on time with five minutes to spare.

As soon as I see him, I instantly say to myself, *damn he is really FINE! I honestly don't remember him being THIS fine.* He was about 200 to 220 lbs of solid muscle; around 6'0 tall and he sported a bald fade with some waves. His smooth dark skin and beautiful brown eyes made him look even better in his Levi's and a nice button up shirt with some square toe shoes. *I wonder did he dress up just for me?*

I walked up and gave him a hug. Damn he smelled good with that Kenneth Cole Black on. He pulled out my chair for me to sit.

"Thanks sir," I smiled.

"So what you been up to lady?" he asked.

"Nothing much," I replied. "Just taking care of business. How about you?"

He pulled his chair closer to the table and said, "Same ole same ole."

I immediately hit him with the Q & A.

"So Kim, what you do again?" He must have known it was coming because he had his replies ready.

"I own two barbershops," he answered. I was legitimately shocked because I didn't remember that.

"Really? Well we have something in common then, because I own a hair salon as well. Where are your shops?"

He smiled, knowing he had peeked my interest.

"I have one in Roseland and the other is in Englewood."

We talked for about 2 hours, just getting to know each other a little better. It turned out to be a very nice lunch. He walked me to my car, opened my door and asked,

"If I call you later will you answer?" He asked with a smile.

"Yes, I promise."

Twenty minutes later, he called.

"Well, it IS later, but I'm more shocked you answered. I'm calling to see if you are free for dinner."

Smiling, I said, "I'm going to the gym at six."

He paused for a second and then said,

"Ok, what about after?"

I ran him my normal routine: "Home, shower and book while in bed."

He wasn't having that.

"Ok how about I come over and cook you dinner then?" He thought he was slick with it. I said to him,

"Kim you just want to come to my house. Wait a minute... you cook?"

"Yes I do," he smiled. He really had me interested then, so I finally relented.

"Yeah sure, come on over. Meet me at my condo on LSD (LakeShore Drive)."

I wasn't about to let him know where I REALLY lived, so I decided to have him meet me at my 'OG Crib' instead.

When I hung, up all I could think was *Lawd what have I done? This man wants to come over and cook. What's his motive? Is he really a nice guy?*

HHD 1

We'll definitely see. His scent was still stuck in my nose. *Let me call the girls and swing by my OG crib. I'mma get an ear full but it's OK. Mom Dukes dying for me to get married and have kids.*

Those heffas were still asleep. I woke their asses right on up.

"Kesh and Lisa, are y'all listening?"

I quickly filled them in on my lunch date and my dinner date plans. Kesh said,

"He's putting in that over time I see."

Then here goess Lisa with her 2 cents,

"Hell she done made him wait 3 months; he has to get to it while he can before she put him on hold again."

"He trying to make you fall in love with his ass. He cooking on the first date/night," Kesh said.

"Kesh girl bye! You a fool," I laughed.

Lisa seemed to be Team Kim all of a sudden, saying, "Just give him a chance Sy."

I knew I was going to take a chance so I said,

"We'll see where this goes. Maybe we can go on some triple dates."

Kesh took the conversation all the way left at this point.

"What if you like him and his sex game weak?"

"I ain't got that far yet. He ain't getting none tonight, so it don't matter. I'll cross that bridge when I get there."

I guess Kesh felt it necessary to remind me of how long it's been, saying, "It's been a year. It'll be sooner than later. It's been a year since you broke up with Harrison ugly ass."

"He was not ugly," I mumbled. "Just an asshole and a ho... Which reminds me, I got to do some research on Kim ass. Check out these barbershops and shit, make sure he's legit 'cause I ain't got time for no BS. I sure hope so 'cause he really is sexy as hell. I hope whenever we do have sex that his dick game is amazing and head game is crazy. I learned my lesson from all these other sideways ass niggas... I'mma call y'all back later. I'm at my OG crib," I told them and hung up.

****

"Mom Dukes! What up?"

My mother is always so happy to see me. "Monie Boo! What up?"

I start smiling 'cause she was cooking and I was hungry, considering I did more talking at lunch than eating.

"Nothing much. Just checking up on you to see if you need to run to the shop before I go to the gym."

She quickly said, "Yeah I do."

"Take your time. When you done cooking, we can leave."

"Nawl...Jane can watch it," she said.

"Ok," I shrugged. "By the way, where IS Jane?"

"She in her office I think," she replied. I pressed the intercom and said,

"J where you at?" I heard her yell, "In the bed."

That ain't like her, so I made my way to the back room where she was and asked,

"Why? Are you sick or something?"

She looked jacked the hell up. "Yeah I think I got pneumonia."

I covered my face and told her "Go your ass to the doctor."

She shivered, saying..

"I did. They gave me some pills and told me to take off a few days."

I laughed 'cause I knew how she hated having to take off work.

"Well you better listen," I chastised her.

"Hey, I need you to run a background check on this guy when you get better."

She tried to smile through her cough and said,

"You finally got a new man, huh?"

I had to pump her breaks.

"Nawl he's just a friend. Here's his info. Now take your sick ass to bed. I will bring mom home after I come from the gym. She needs her hair done baaaaadd. Love ya Bye."

****

Once I dropped Ma Dukes back home, I went to the crib and decided to take a nice bath. I needed to relax for a minute and get my thoughts together. *Lord, I'm going to give him a chance, cuz I sure do miss the company. Hell, I'm 30 and single. I don't do drama and my life is going great....just no man. I'mma take it slow until after Jane run his background check.* My cell rang, interrupting my thoughts. *Damn, I bet this him calling.*

"Hello?"

"Yes. I'm just trying to see if you are home yet."

I dried my hands, trying hard not to drop the phone in the tub. "Yeah I'm here."

I could tell he was shocked I answered the phone. He said,

"Ok I'll be there in 20 minutes. I'm leaving the store now."

Just then, Kesh beeped in.

"Ok this is my friend on my other line. See you when you get here."

"Kesh what up?" I said, clicking over.

She dived right in with the questions.

"So are you going to give him some or not?"

I had the ugly face when I said, "Hell no. I'm good."

"You said he's nice, right?" she reiterated.

"Ok?? What the hell that mean?" I dared her.

"It's just too early to have sex with him."

She hit me with, "Girl you grown! You can do whatever the hell you want. Ain't nobody gon' judge you."

She almost had me with her logic, but I decided to shut this conversation down real quick.

"Ok girl, he's almost here. I'll call you tonight or in the morning. Byeeee."

Just as I was heading back down the stairs, the bell rings.

"Heyyy," I smiled at Kim as I opened the door for him.

"Welcome to my home. The kitchen is this way. So what are you about to cook?"

"I was thinking since you just came from the gym, I'd prepare us something lite," he replied as he set the groceries on the counter top. How does a crumbled blue cheese salad with a vinaigrette dressing and croutons on the side sound?"

I cracked up laughing. "Too funny. I see you listen when I talk."

He winked. "Yes, I do. Where are your wine glasses?"

I pointed and replied, "Over the sink."

He poured us each a glass of Moscato and handed me one.

"Here…sip on this til I get this masterpiece together."

Ha-ha…masterpiece huh?

"This is a nice place you have," he complimented.

I looked around as if the house wasn't mine and replied, "Thanks."

Something must have peeked his interest because he then asked, "Who decorated?"

I looked at him like, duh....who else? But instead I just said, "I did."

He quickly said, "You need to come decorate mine."

Flattered, I told him, "You just want me at your house."

"Yeah that too," Kim laughingly admitted, "but I really do need something done 'cause it's very 'plain Jane' over there."

I quickly changed the subject. "So what's the name of your shops?"

He smiled; he knew what I was doing. He went along with it and replied,

"*Kutz*. So Symone, tell me what you like to do for fun."

I thought for a minute, then I shot him off a list.

"I love the Bulls and the Bears. I go to all the games with my friends. They use it as man-hunting nights but I actually LOVE the games. I also like skating and bowling. I like watching movies. Oh and I love to SHOP."

He looked impressed when I mentioned the Bulls and the Bears.

"I've never known a woman who loves sports."

I sipped my wine and coyly replied, "Well you know one now."

I was shocked when he said, "Well let's go to the next game….my treat."

I had to let him know I peeped his game.

"You just want another date. Besides…I'm a season ticket holder already."

Kim grabbed his chest and laughed.

"Well in THAT case, the next game can be YOUR treat and I'll treat us to bowling Friday. That's what I like to do. And now, dinner is served."

I looked at the beautiful bowl of salad he placed in front of me. This looks good! I wonder does it taste as good as it looks.

"Let me refill your glass," he offered.

"Are you trying to get me drunk?" I asked him, as I began going through my collection of DVD's,

He chuckled and took a seat on the couch. "No ma'am. So what movie are we watching?"

I told him one of my favorites, " In Too Deep."

He seemed impressed by that as well but shook his head and replied,

"Ok Ok. But Scarface is the best movie out."

He didn't know me very well yet so I excused him and let him know, "Oh I got that to."

He gave me a thumbs up and said, "I really like you now, Symone."

I feigned shock. "Oh Really? And all it took was my movie selection. Now THAT was easy."

"I wonder how easy it'll be to make you fall in love with me," he whispered.

I had no words; I just snuggled up closer to him on the couch, where we ate, drank some more wine and watched the movie til we both passed out.

****

I woke glancing up at the clock on the wall; 3:45 am. Kim was sound asleep on the other end of the couch. *Damn*, I thought, *he even sleeps fine*. I grew instantly wet. Without giving it a second thought, I climbed on his lap and began kissing him and nibbling his ear, whispering, "It's been awhile baby, and I'm long overdue."

He immediately grabbed my breast with a nice firm grip, pulling my hair and kissing me so hard and passionately, I could feel my juices flowing. He kissed me all over my neck and chest. I felt my nipples grow harder and harder. He's kissing me harder, deeper, like he's wanting this just as much as I do.

I unbuttoned his shirt, kissing down his chest. When I reached his belt, I began to unbuckle his pants and just as I was going to take him in my mouth, he stopped me, kissed me again, and picked me up moaning, "Show me to the bedroom."

He laid me on the bed and began to massage my body so good. As his hands expertly roamed every inch of me, all I could think was what he would feel like inside of me. This massage felt so good, it's like he was fucking me mentally, and it was feeling so good emotionally.

Suddenly, he flipped me over and began to suck on my toes and lick up my inner thigh. I felt a small shiver go through me. Once he reached my lips again, he gave me another long, passionate kiss. I drifted off into heaven. He climbed on the side of me and begin to massage the front of me. He started with my hands, moved up my arms then made his way across my shoulders. I knew I deserved all of this, but couldn't understand why he was doing it, so I just lay there and enjoyed it. Once he reached my mid-area, I had creamed on myself at least twice already. I could feel myself drifting back to sleep. I sure was tired, but didn't want to be rude, so I fought it as long as I could. I mean damn, he had me feeling so loose and relaxed you would've thought he was a certified, bona-fied massage therapist. Sadly, the next thing I know, my eyes got heavy and I guess I drifted right back to sleep.

****

When I awoke again, it was 12:30 pm. Kim was still asleep, stretched out on the recliner. I was in the bed with the covers over me. He had my top blanket on him. He looked so peaceful. I respected him even more now because he didn't take advantage of the situation, but my body was craving it more now that his hands had been all over me.

I went to the kitchen and made us a breakfast of eggs, toast and sausage with OJ. I woke him up and told him there was a toothbrush on the sink and breakfast was waiting for him once he was done. He smiled and said..

"I can definitely get used to this."

I looked backed and seductively smiled at him. "I bet you could."

As I started to clean the kitchen, he walked up behind, wrapped his strong arms around my waist and whispered, "I see you know how to treat a man."

"I sure do," I replied. "Question is though....does the man know how to treat me?"

He spun me around and kissed me, lifting up me on top of the counter. He pulled my pants down, admired my perfectly shaved pussy, and hungrily licked his lips. As soon as his tongue found his way inside my walls, I threw my head back and moaned....yes lawd.

The first two licks felt like heaven. He licked me, sucked me and tongue fucked me til I came over and over and over again. I felt that big orgasm building up. I grabbed the back of his head and released all my waterfall; he happily licked it right on up. I quickly hopped down from the counter and told him..

"You are on the right track, but sex isn't what I was talking about."

But at the same time…damn! At this point, all I can think is how crazy his head game is. *I definitely have to test drive that mouth again.*

We both got dressed, leaving the house. I could feel him watching me as I strolled to my car, so I swayed my hips just a little harder. He opened my door for me and helped me in. As I drove, my only thoughts were of the night before and just this morning. ***Jesus please let him be Mr. Right. Lord knows I have had my share of Mr. Wrongs and Mr. Wasted My Damn Time. I am too damn old for to continue down that road…ain't nobody got time for that!***

KIM

"This K. What up?"

"Dawg!" his little brother, Sam, bellowed into the phone.

"Where you at? You know we got that meeting at 4."

"Yeah I know. I'll be there at 3:45," I assured him.

"It's Friday bro, chill out. I'm always on my business. I just got back to the crib; let me hop in the shower. I'll hit you back when I'm on the way."

I heard the shock in my brother's voice.

"You JUST pulling up to your crib?! Where you been all night?"

I shut the conversation down quick.

"Bye foolie. That's my business."

I have a 3br/3bath house in the Tinley Park area: beautiful marble counter tops, stainless steel everything and a sectional. The ONLY issue I have is it desperately needs a woman's touch...BAD.

As soon as I hopped in the shower, I immediately flashback to Symone and last night. *Damn...she just might be the one. We shall see.*

I quickly finish my shower and throw on some black slacks and a lilac button up with some black pointed toe shoes. I slid my wrist through the band of my platinum watch by Jacob the Jeweler and hit my chest with that new Jay Z cologne. I called my brother to let him know I was on the way and shot Sy a quick text, just to let her know she was deep on my mind.

Me: "Hey lady. Just letting you know I enjoyed all of yesterday and to see if we still on for tonight."
Sy: "Yes :) Where are we bowling?"
Me: "Brunswick in Homewood, but let's grab a bite to eat first. I'll text you the place later."
Sy: "Ok ttyl"

It was 3:45 on the dot. *Damn I'm good.*

"What up Sam?" he greeted as he strolled into the office.

"Told you I'm always on time. So let's get down to business. Who we gotta take out to get what we want since they don't want to act right?"

"K, we businessmen now…that's supposed to be a last resort," Sam reminded him.

"Nawl bro," K shook his head in disagreement.

"In this business you have to show them who boss."

"Calm down bro. We ARE showing them…just in a different way. We're going to make them an offer they can't refuse," Sam said in his Don Corleone voice, laughing a little.

K completely ignored his brother's Godfather reference.

"Man fuck that! Tell Paul's little helpers if they don't launder my money and get it back to me CLEAN at 15%, I'm going to take out his whole family and make him watch! I ain't get here being fucking nice."

Sam regarded his brother very long and hard for a few seconds.

"K, have you ever thought about getting out? Bro, we already rich. We need to sit back and get out scott free. This shit is stressful and people acting crazy and money hungry."

K nodded his head in agreement. "I'm definitely thinking about it."

Suddenly, Sam remembered K never answered his earlier question, so he asked again.

"Oh yeah, where were you last night? I called you all night to see if you wanted to go to the Island Bar."

K smiled and said, "I finally got up with that chick I've been trying to hook up with for the past three months and prepared dinner for her."

Sam was shocked. "Wait, wait…you cooked?!"

K laughed.

"Why the hell do people keep saying that? Yes I did and you know I can cook. While we ate, we watched **In Too Deep**, then we fell asleep."

Sam stared at him.

"After all that, you fell sleep? No action….no nothing?"

K smiled at his brother, mainly because he was shocked his damn self.

"Nawl bro. It ain't even like that. She's one of 'them.' She really got her shit together. She even owns her own business. If this goes how I want it to, I'll definitely get out the game for her."

BZZZ!!

"Mr. P is here," Sheila the receptionist buzzed in.

"Let him in please," Sam instructed.

Mr. P strutted in with the confidence of 2 peacocks. "K and Sam! My two favorite people!"

"Cut the shit Pablo!" K spat.

"Are you going to handle my money or do I need to go elsewhere?"

Pablo shook his head.

"I don't need the feds and all the other peoples all over my business. I run my shit legit and I want it to still be that way when you're done."

"I just need this 2 million and I'm out. You'll get your 10% and then we done. Don't cross me bruh; I have NO problem sending my boy to see your mom."

Pablo nervously threw his hands up.

"Ok Ok! No need for all that."

"So when can I expect it?" K pressured.

"Give me a month."

"Tru dat," K accepted. "You know where to find me. I'll send someone over with the money tomorrow. Sam see him out."

When Sam re-entered the office, he was almost doubled over in laughter.

"Damn Bro he was scared as hell!"

"You got to put fear in them or they will try to fuck you over," K calmly explained.

"I guess," Sam shrugged, shaking his head. "But anyway....back to last night! So this chick got you cooking and shit?"

"Nawl how bout we get to what happened when you went to that game," K said, turning the tables on his brother.

Sam smiled and rubbed his chin.

"Yo I met three FINE ass women and got a few numbers. I'mma see if I can go out tonight with one of them. Shit, I need a wife. I want to get out the game; settle down; raise a family and shit."

"Word up!" K agreed, dapping up his brother. He checked his timepiece and quickly rose from his seat.

"Yo, I gotta go get ready for my date. She doesn't know THIS side of me; she only know 'barbershop K.'"

Sam smiled and said, "Damn Bro, are you in love already? That must've been some dinner."

K blushed a little at the mention of the 'L' word.

"Nawl, not in love just yet...just happy. She puts a smile on my face and don't even know it."

"That's wussup!" Sam grinned, patting his brother on the back.

"Just be careful though....that last bitch tried to do you in." K thought about it and replied

"Yeah," K said, allowing his mind to flashback to his last relationship. "She damn sure tried to."

****

SYMONE

"Kesh….where are you?" I inquired.

"At the store," she stated matter-of-factly. "Someone has to open it up."

"Ok….be there in five."

As soon as I hung up, my phone dinged with an incoming text…

K: "Are you down for pizza and beer for dinner?"

Symone: "Yeah that's cool."

K: "Beggars in Oak Forest at 5:30"

Symone: "See you there."

Damn I can't stop smiling thinking about him and last night.

****

"What up Jane? What you got for me?"

"He had a record but it's been sealed," Jane explained.

"He owns two shops; never been married; no kids. Oh and he got a nice inheritance from his grandma."

I waited two beats, expecting Jane to load me up with more info. When she didn't, I huffed,

"That's it?"

"Yes ma'am," she confirmed.

was shocked, but accepted the info graciously.

"Ok, thanks a ton beautiful."

"Hey, I need a FYE jumpsuit for tonight," Jane said coyly.

"I thought you were sick heffa," I laughed.

"I'm good now," she giggled. "It's ladies night tonight."

"Ok," I chuckled, shaking my head. "Just swing on by the shop and I'll lay you out a few things."

Jane girly-squealed ever so slightly.

"Ok! Soon as Shika hooks me up, I'll be thru there."

****

"Kesh, come to the office girl," I said grabbing her by the arm as I breezed through the boutique.

"Liz, can you watch the store for us please? And pull some one-piece jump suits for Jane. She'll be stopping by later."

"Sure girl. I got you," Liz agreed smiling.

As soon as I shut the door to my office, I released all of my giddiness on Kesh.

"Giiiiiiirl! The things Kim did with his mouth was AMAZING! I ain't had it like THAT in a WHILE!"

Kesh was so happy, you'd have thought SHE just got her some. "I knew it!" she squealed.

I had to stop her in her tracks.

"Hold it now....we did NOT have sex; he just massaged my whole body til I fell asleep."

Kesh just stared at me for a split second, then smiled. "Damn, he got you all glowing and shit."

"Shut up heffa," I blushed.

As I gave Kesh all of my juicy blow-by-blow details, she grew more and more excited.

"Damn bitch," she exhaled, fanning herself, "you got me all hot and bothered now. Good thing I got a date tonight."

"With who?" I asked, cocking my eyebrow at her.

"With Sam," she sing-songed.

"Oh...the one from the game?"

"Yup....the one you said looks like Tyrese. He cool peoples. We've been talking on the phone and he finally asked me out, so I'm down. We had drinks Tuesday, but this is a REAL date. He owns his own clothing store called Apparel Unlimited."

She paused for a brief moment. "I want to see what he about. Shit I may need to call Jane," she half-laughed.

"I refuse to be used and abuse again."

"Well..." I said, trying to lighten the mood after a slightly awkward silence, "let's do these books cuz I got a date in about hour or so too."

"I hope you ain't booked over into our Saturday Morning catch up," she warned.

"No," I assured her, "it's just bowling and pizza. What are you and Lisa bringing so I can know what I need to bring?"

"Lisa's bringing drinks."

"Tell her don't forget my lemonade," I reminded her.

"I won't," Kesh promised. "And I got breakfast."

"Ok cool. Girl, we made some money this month!" I said excitedly, switching the convo back to business.

"I ordered some nice pieces this week."

"We got them in already," Kesh informed me. "Girl, I'm so glad we're in business together and that YOU do the books."

"Bitch don't get all sentimental now," I laughed. "I have to get dressed."

"What are you wearing?"

I didn't even know. I shrugged my shoulders, saying, "I know there's something cute in this store."

****

Later that evening, Lisa's nosy ass texted me:

Lisa: "What up ma?"

Me: "Nothing much....trying to find something to wear on this date."

Lisa: "Another date? He putting in that work I see"

Me: "Shut up."

Lisa: "He going to have you sprung...watch."

Me: "Nawl imma have HIS head gone. What you been up to? I'll be at shop in a min to pick up the deposit on my way bowling."

Lisa: "Ok and nothing, I have been kicking it with this lil fine ass girl."

Me: "Damn where you find her?"

Lisa: "Shit, she was staring me down in the grocery store and it went from there."

Me: "I heard that. Have you hit yet?"

Lisa: "Nope Y do you want to watch?"

Me:" Hell yeah. I see you in 10 mins lol."

Next, I shot Kim a quick text:

Me: "Be there in 30mins"

K: "Ok"

Then I texted Jane:

Me: "Kesh and Lisa pulled you out some jumpers."

Jane: "Ok I'm on my way now. You should meet us at the Dolphin after your date."

Me: "I'll swing thru. Let me see if Kesh can come too."

Jane: "Cool!"

HHD 1

As soon as I pulled up to the restaurant, I quickly checked my makeup in the visor and touched up my lip gloss. I was looking TOO fine in this Sheem'a off the shoulder shirt and shorts with my black Red Bottom boots. I got out the car, turned my excitement down a notch and walked in.

As I move through the restaurant, every head turned in my direction. I knew I looked good and K happily told me so.

"Damn you look sexy as hell ma!"

Smiling hard as hell, I managed to squeeze out,

"Thanks....you're looking handsome yourself."

"Well you know I try," he smiled as he embraced me. His scent immediately hit my nose.

Mmmm....Is that Jay Z I smell?"

He smiled so big I said, "I'll take that as a yes."

Once we were seated, we ordered our food, ate and talked for what seemed like hours. I almost forgot how good this felt. He was so nice and sweet, asking me about my day, making me feel as if it was all about me. I didn't want to control the entire conversation though so I said, "Ok enough about me…how was your day?"

With a pleased look on his face he said,"I cut a few good heads."

"So you got good clientele then?" I asked, intrigued.

"Yeah," he nodded, smiling. "I do ok."

He looked happy talking about his business so I continued. "It seems you love what you do."

"I do indeed," he confirmed.

"On another note, I really need you to come decorate my house."

I laughed. "Ok, ok. Even though I KNOW you just want me in your house sir."

"I really want to have a party, but it's not decorated properly," he frowned.

"Ok then…let's make a deal," I negotiated. "If you cook, I will come."

"Shit, baby I'll cook lunch AND dinner!" he laughed.

"Deal!" I grinned.

"Now, you ready to get whupped?" I asked, grabbing my purse.

He laughed. "After you, my lady."

HHD 1

We decided to go to Oak Forest bowling alley, right down the street from the restaurant. As we laced up our shoes, he quietly asked, "So...when are you going to let me be your man?"

"Hmmm... let me think," I said, stalling just a little. "Do you think you're ready?"

He huffed, "What do you think?"

"When you going to let me see the real you K?" I challenged.

"What you see is what you get baby," he rather smugly replied.

"You better focus on this game," I said, redirecting the conversation.

"I don't want no excuses when I win. I see you must make damn good money cutting hair, driving that car you got and living in TP."

"I can say the same about you with that condo," he swung back.

I do alright," I agreed. "As matter of fact, I have a house and a condo."

"Damn you a baller!" he laughed.

"Nawl," I said, shaking my head. "Just a businesswoman with a shoe and purse fetish."

"Oh really?" he said, cocking his right eyebrow, "What a coincidence….I have a jean and Jordan fetish. So then tell me….what do you see when you look at a guy like me?"

"Hmm…let me think on that one." I stared at him for a moment, allowing myself at least 15, 20 seconds to really dig deep into his soul.

"I see a man who hides pain but he enjoys life. I also see how close you are to your mother or grandmother cuz you know how to treat a woman."

He smiled and slowly nodded his head, impressed. "Well you're off to a good start. I'm an honest man; I don't believe in cheating or hitting a woman. I love hard, but it seems to always be the wrong person, and I HATE BEING TAKEN FOR GRANTED. Soooo….is there anything I should know about you?"

"Know that I'm beating you in this game," I laughed as he chuckled, shaking his head.

"But seriously though, I'm a simple girl. I like simple things in life. I HATE LIARS. I enjoy every moment of my life; I have two godchildren. I'm a momma's girl; I have two best friends and I'm proud that I own my own businesses. What turns me on is giving head and a man who knows what he wants out of life. The rest…you will have to learn on you own."

"Damn," he gushed, "you like sports and giving head?! Will you marry me?"

****

"So what are you about to do now?" he asked, walking me to my car.

"I'm bout to slide over to The Dolphin to hang out with my sis for a little while."

"Oh, you going clubbing?"

"Yeah, you want to come? Since you my MAN and all," I smiled, batting my eyelashes at him.

He laughed. "Nawl, I'm good. Go do you boo. If you don't mind, just gimme your key and I'll meet you at your crib when you are done."

"It's a key-less entry, but I got a "catch-up" with my girls in the morning. On Saturday mornings they come to my spot and we watch all the TV shows we missed all week."

"Oh, I'll be gone by the time they get there," he assured me.

"You sure about that, Mr. Sleepy Head?" I laughed.

"You got jokes I see," he chuckled.

"How about you just wait til Sunday?" I suggested. "Then you can have me all day."

He pulled me close and whispered, "How about I have you today and Sunday?"

"Ok," I finally relented. "Call me when you get there so I can give you the code to get you in."

"Damn....my baby a baller! You got all the up to date shit!"

"Nawl, I just like nice top-notch shit. I spoil myself cuz I don't have no one else to do it."

"Well, you got me now baby."

"Well heyyy now," I smiled. "We shall see."

"I got you," K whispered in my ear. "I promise Symone I will never hurt you."

****

As I get out the car, I see Kesh.

"The Dolphin is jumping tonight! It's packed!"

She pointed to the sign. "That's cuz it's reggae night. You know this my favorite. Let me get my whine on!"

When we stepped inside, it was like trying to squeeze into a can of sardines.

"Damn! We can barely move in this bitch! Let's try to find Jane." I allowed my eyes to scan the circumference of the club until I finally spotted her.

"Found her!" I yelled, grabbing Kesh's arm.

"Hang on a sec," she paused. "My phone is vibrating like crazy."

Sam: "Can I taste that tonight?"

Kesh: "Sure can boo"

Sam: "Meet me in an hour at my crib."

Kesh: "Send me the address. I'll be there."

We maneuvered our way through the packed floor, finally reaching the table where Jane was waiting for us. After about 2 hours of being able to do nothing more than people watch and fan ourselves with napkins because it was so damn packed and so damn hot in there, I'd had enough.

"That's it. I'm done. I'm ret' ta go!"

Kesh couldn't have been happier.

"Yeeeesss! Now I can go get me some dick!"

"Shit me 2," Jane said, snapping her fingers.

"Well hell me 3," I added, laughing."

"Damn shame we all getting dick and Lisa getting pussy," Kesh giggled.

I whipped out my phone to show them the picture that Lisa sent me of her new girlfriend.

"This is what she looks like. Shit even I want to hit that!"

"Did you tell Kim you like girls?" Kesh asked me, cocking her eyebrow.

"Nope I want to surprise him," I giggled.

"Oh honey he's going to marry yo ass after that…watch!"

I just smiled.

****

Kim met me at the door…naked. He pulled me inside, passionately kissing me as he shut the door behind me. He began taking off my clothes and as I slid out of my shoes he stopped me.

"No leave them on. I love to see you in heels."

Once I was completely naked, except for my shoes, of course, he said, "Close your eyes. I have a surprise for you."

He guided me to the already running shower, taking off my heels after he walked behind me, watching. He washed my entire body from head to toe, then gave me a plush terry cloth robe to put on. When he opened the bedroom door, it was covered in candle light with rose pedals everywhere.

"Awwww, this is beautiful!" I swooned. "Did you do all this while I was in the shower? And who told you I love white roses?"

"I pay attention, remember?" he said, softly kissing my lips. He then laid me across the bed and began massaging my feet, shoulders and neck like an expert. It was absolute heaven, and we talked into the wee hours of the morning, until we finally fell asleep, wrapped in each other's arms.

****

"Well shit Sy," Lisa huffed at me when I finally opened the door for her the next morning.

"I've been calling your ass all night,"

My bad man," I apologized. "I must've left my phone down here somewhere."

"Mmmm hmmm," she said, rolling her eyes and looking around the room.

"Damn bitch…you had fun last night with all these roses and shit?"

"All we did was talk while he rubbed my feet and massaged my shoulders and back."

"Damn he treating you damn good! I'm getting jealous," she teased. "And he cooked breakfast TOO? It's still hot!"

"Awww," I gushed. "He must've have done all of this before he left. Oh, he left me a note." I read it to myself:

Hey boo,

I hope you enjoyed last night. There's definitely more nights like this to come. I told you I'll spoil you. All our nights don't have to be about sex. I cooked y'all breakfast; I hope you enjoy your day. Text me later and I'll see you tomorrow. I left you a key and the address to my crib... K

I didn't even realize I was giggling and smiling from ear-to-ear until I looked up from the letter and saw Lisa staring at me, smirking. I cleared my throat and shook off my giddiness.

"Ummm….where's Kesh? Shouldn't she be here by now?"

"She texted me while you were getting lost in your love letter," Lisa drawled. "She said she'll be here in about 5 minutes."

"Cool. That gives me just enough time to wash up right quick and brush my teeth," I said dashing into the bathroom.

I could barely brush my teeth properly for smiling so hard as I thought about the previous evening and how thoughtful he was to get up early enough this morning to prepare me and my girls breakfast. Now I have to return the favor to him….show him what a REAL woman should do for her man.

****

When I arrived at Kim's house the next day, I walked right inside, smiling to myself because I was able to use MY key he'd given me. I immediately heard the shower running, so I knew where he was. Since he was preoccupied with his shower, I decided to have me a look around his crib and see what all I needed to do.

He has a nice big living room and kitchen; now let me check out these bedrooms. Empty all three of them, including his. Oh wait, excuse me…he DOES have a California king size bed in there. I was blown away. When he said his place needed a "woman's touch," he ain't never lied.

"Ummm….baby?" I yelled through the bathroom door.

"S'up love?" he said, as he turned off the faucet.

"Your place needs A LOT of help….and it's definitely gonna cost you," I laughed.

"Woooow….so you're gonna charge me?" he laughed as well.

"Boy please…the miracle I'mma have to work up in here, you wouldn't be able to afford my fee," I said cracking up laughing.

"So all I need from you is your credit card so I can handle my business tomorrow."

He stepped out of the bathroom, in all his chocolaty glory, with nothing but a towel wrapped around his waist. I swear I think I may have drooled a little. He pulled his wallet out of his pants' pocket and passed me his Black American Express card.

"This should allow you to do everything you need to baby," he said as he pressed his still damp body against mine and kissed me. *Oh yeah*, I thought to myself *this is gonna be well worth it.*

****

The next day I used his card and got straight to work, purchasing furniture for every room in his house. I started off with the living room, getting him an all-white leather love seat, couch and recliner with ottoman, along with a beautiful coffee table set by Maitland-Smith.

Then I moved on to the man cave, which is really only one of the bedrooms, but I hooked it up as if it was for me, since I'm such a die-hard sports fan. I decorated it in Bears, Blackhawks and of course Bulls accessories. I also grabbed him a 50-inch TV for the wall; a mini bar and fridge; and ordered a black leather sofa, two recliners and some end tables.

The final room was done in a neutral color, since this will be his guest bedroom. I made it very homey, decorating it with a 42-inch TV for the wall and a beautiful oak wood bedroom set from Ashley Furniture. I definitely did my thang if I do say so myself. *Now to finish this kitchen and the dining room. After all this, AND a two day wait on this furniture, I need to go relax in a tub. I am beyond tired. Oh yes honey, he's going to owe me big time for all this here! I may have to get myself a new Chanel bag and a pair of Jimmy Choo's or something on him.*

After my bath, I decided to rest up on his new couch and watch Scarface with some popcorn and my favorite lemonade.

HHD 1

SYMONE

K and I were celebrating our 1-year anniversary. We decided not to go anywhere, opting instead to just stay home, relax in front of the fireplace and enjoy each other's company over some Chinese food and Think Like a Man 2. Little did he know, this evening was about to take a VERY interesting turn.

At 10:00 on the dot, the doorbell rang.

Kim jerked his head towards the wall clock and gave me a quizzical look.

"Who in the world could that be?"

just smiled. "I guess we're about to find out."

When I walked back into the living room, I was hand-in-hand with a beautiful 5'9, 175lb curvalicious, chocolate skin toned Amazon. The look of confusion on Kim's face was priceless.

"Baby, this is Mel. Mel this is K."

"Hello K," Mel cooed.

"Hi," K answered her, giving me a "what the fuck" look.

As he continued to silently question me, Mel turned her attention back to me.

"So what you been up to boo? It's been a long time."

"Nothing just running the business," I replied. "I've missed you."

"Prove it," Mel demanded, as she intertwined her fingers in my hair and yanked my head back.

We kissed passionately and began to paw all over each other, she massaging my breasts and kneading my nipples between her fingers; me squeezing and rubbing her apple shaped ass.

I stole a quick glance at K and his jaw was literally on the floor, not to mention his dick was standing at FULL attention. I pulled away from Mel and held my hand out to K.

"Well don't just stand there baby....come help me make OUR date feel welcome." K cocked his eyebrow at the mention of the words "our date."

"Seriously?" he asked, darting his eyes back and forth between us.

"Seriously," I confirmed, and threw my tongue down his throat to further convince him. And from that precise moment, shit was on and poppin'!

We immediately laid him down and I climbed on top of his face as Mel began to give him head. I never get enough of his tongue and I know he was getting pleased from Mel cuz her head game was off the chain.

After K made me cum a few times, I dismounted his face and Mel and I double-teamed his dick. As she sucked his rod, I licked his balls, then we'd switch up. He seemed to be in heaven, what with all the moaning he was doing.

Then Mel climbed on top of him and began riding him slowly as I sat back and played with my kitten. I got off just watching them. This kind of stuff always excites me. Once Mel made K cum, she attached her strap-on and fucked me doggy-style as I went back to giving K some top-notch head. I'd always held back cuz I knew this day was coming, so he could barely breathe as he muttered..

"Damn bae! You ain't ever did it like this!"

I sucked him harder and faster, all while taking them 9 inches from the back. K was speechless. His eyes rolled in the back of his head and just when he was about to cum, I stopped.

"No no not yet!"

I glanced over my shoulder and watched Mel as she plowed into my pussy from behind.

"Damn Mel this shit is the bomb," I gasped.

She pumped into me a few times, then pulled out so I could climb on top of K backwards and as I bounced my juicy ass on top of his dick, I gave Mel some head, as I make sure I always do. We continued pumping and bouncing and licking and sucking and fucking until suddenly, we all came back-to-back; first Mel, then me and finally K. We all tumbled apart from each other and collapsed on the bed, soaking in the afterglow. Mel fell asleep at the foot of the bed and I slid up and lay my head on K's chest. I gave him one more passion-filled kiss and stared lovingly into his eyes as I said.

"Happy Anniversary baby."

****

Mel left in the wee hours of the morning. K and I must've been in deep sleep because neither of us heard her leave.

The next day, as we lounged around the house, K and I reminisced over the previous evening's festivities.

"Damn that was the best gift I ever got!" he gushed. "I didn't know you like women."

"Yeah I love women."

"You sleep with her all the time?"

"Every blue moon, but not since you and I have been together. She was on strike," I laughed.

"Damn….you got anything else you need to tell me?" K asked suspiciously.

"Nope. That was my only secret and I wanted to save it for a special occasion…THIS occasion."

"Ooooo weeee baby," he smiled at me as he wrapped my hands in his and kissed them.

"That's what the fuck I'm talking about right there! One time and I'm already hooked! Just let me have a piece of the action every now and then and I'm good!"

"Hmmm….I'm sure we can work that out," I giggled coyly.

****

The next day felt like I was sleepwalking through a dream. Even now, I'm blown away by how the day transpired. First, K surprised the hell out of me with a brand new CAR; a 2016 pink champagne colored BMW X6 with yet another surprise awaiting me on the driver seat; a Blue

Pitball puppy. But even THAT wasn't all! Around the puppy's neck was a blue velvet box, and when K removed it, he dropped to one knee and removed the contents of it: a Gia Certified Bulgari Platinum 3.00ct diamond engagement ring. My heart literally skipped a beat.

"Sy….this last year with you has been amazing. I don't know what I did to deserve somebody as wonderful as you in my life, but I'll be damned if I'll ever let you go. Baby, I love you more than words can ever say, so I hope this ring proves that I want to be yours forever. Symone…will you marry me?"

I could barely see him to wrap my arms around him. I wasn't crying a river…it was more like a flood.

"Yes baby!" I squealed. "Yes yes yes yes yes yes!!" He slid the ring on my finger and we kissed like two lovesick teenagers. Suddenly, he pulled away from me.

"C'mon…let's get ready to go out."

"Um…ok," I agreed, completely flustered. "But I don't have anything to wear here."

He gave me sneaky smile.

"No worries baby. Ya man has everything covered. Go check the guest bedroom."

When I opened the door to the bedroom, I thought I was stepping into the showroom at Neiman Marcus. He had every style, cut and color of dress; every designer shoe and purse to match; designer jewelry and accessories; and a vanity table spread from end-to-end with all of my favorite makeup from MAC. *Oh my God*, I thought to myself, *my boo has really outdone himself.*

****

"K…oh my God!" I exclaimed. "Why are we at the airport?"

"My mans let me borrow his jet for the night," he replied,

"Oh my God!" I started giggling uncontrollably. "So where we going?"

"It's a surprise," he laughed.

"Wow," I gushed. "This day couldn't possibly get any better than this!"

"Oh yes it can baby," K laughed, disagreeing. "Trust me."

Forty minutes later, we were in Vegas! I could NOT believe it!

As soon as we departed the plane, we stepped into a silver stretch limo, where we were whisked away to the Bellagio Hotel. I followed him into the casino and played for about four hours, winning about $2000 at the Poker and Roulette tables.

We took the elevator up to the Presidential Suite, where we had a dinner of steak, shrimp and asparagus waiting for us, along with caramel truffle cheesecake for dessert and 2 bottles of champagne chilling on ice. I was floored and impressed at all the thought he put into this.

At the same time, I was also like *damn, where the hell did he get the money to pay for all of this? This shit is NOT cheap!* I quickly put the questions out of my head. It didn't even matter at that point.

All I knew and cared about was that I had a man who was spoiling the hell out of ME for a change and I loved it! I threw my arms around his neck and kissed him long and hard.

"Thank you K," I said, smiling from ear-to-ear.

"Thank you so much for giving me the best day of my life."

HHD 1

"Nawl baby," he said, looking down at me. "You haven't seen your BEST day yet. There's so much more to come."

****

HHD 1

KIM

"POLICE!! WE GOT A SEARCH WARRANT!! EVERYONE PUT YOUR HANDS UP...NOW!!"

K was shocked.

"What are y'all searching for?"

The police ignored him and continued to usher everyone outside.

"This some bullshit! Where is my copy of the warrant?" K demanded.

"Damn bro...what are they searching for?" one of the customers asked.

"It says drugs, money, any bank statements and all shop paperwork," K read off the list.

"They ain't got shit on us. If they did, we'd all be in cuffs right now. This is just a scare tactic. We'll be back in a few hours. Yo Al...watch the shop for me."

****

Down at the station, the police told me they had massive evidence against me for drug trafficking and money laundering. Inside, I was scared shitless but I wasn't about to let them see me sweat.

"I just want my phone call....no more no less."

"Well maybe we will go pick up your brother and ask him," they threatened.

I didn't even bat an eyelid.

"Go ahead. Lawyer....that's all I want."

"Ok...guess that means this conversation is done. Just ponder on this while you make your call. Who you think told us about you?"

"L-A-W-Y-E-R," I repeated exaggeratedly.

Both officers stared at me for about 5 seconds before finally escorting me down the hall to where the phone booths were located. I was concerned about my shop, so the first call I made was to check on it.

"Al how bad did they tear up the shop?

"They really did a number on it," Al sighed.

"Damn! Do you think we can have it right by tomorrow?"

"Yeah they really ain't damage nothing....just gonna take a lot of clean up."

"Cool. They ain't read me no rights or nothing so I know I'll be out of here in a minute. I will call you if I need bail so you and Sam be on stand by to get my debit card and run to the bank".

****

The next day I told Symone to meet me at the shop. Those pigs really did work my shop over and when Sy walked in and looked around, her surprise at the condition of it was evident.

"Baby! What the hell happened up in here?"

"The police raided us. I may need Jane to represent me in whatever case they say they got against me."

"Wait…what?" she asked, completely confused.

"Why would they raid your shop K?"

"Here…this is what they gave me," I said, handing her the charge list.

"It says drugs and money laundering," she read, still shaking her head in confusion.

"Why the hell would they think you're laundering money K?"

I took a deep breath and looked into her beautiful browns.

"Because I am baby. Right now, I'm cleaning my last hundred mil; another 8 months and I'm out the game."

"Hold the fuck up….you what?!" Sy screamed.

"Why the fuck didn't you tell me all this before? Didn't I tell you I despise liars?"

If I'd hung my head any lower, I think it would've popped off my neck and rolled onto the floor. It killed me to see her so hurt and know that I was the cause of her pain.

"I just didn't want you to be involved in all this shit," I explained to her. "Then they would've been all up in your house and your shops fucking shit up. You're clean…I just wanted you to stay that way."

"K, if they've been watching YOU all this damn time, I can almost guarantee they know who I am by now," she spat. "Well that definitely explains how we've been able to do all this traveling and shopping and whatnot. Cuz I sure was wondering where the hell you were getting all this money from."

"I'm wise with my money," I explained to her. "I use it wisely and I don't go spending it foolishly."

I took a deep breath.

"Listen, Sy…you know I would never do anything to hurt you. I promise you…we're going to get through all of this. But the first thing I need to do is find who's the bitch snitch in my fucking circle…"

****

Six long months had passed and would you believe these bitch ass cops were STILL harassing me? And because they had absolutely nothing else to pull out of their "bag of tricks," they continued threatening me with calling in my brother. They're so stupid. Didn't they know that blood is 10 times thicker than water? My brother ain't got shit to tell them and I made sure I let them know that. But the beautiful thing is we no longer have to worry about this mess because just when things were really about to get heated, in swoops Jane and she shuts that shit DOWN! Told them anything else they need to know about anything else should be addressed to HER and ONLY her. It was awesome! Those pigs choked down whatever was about to come out of their mouths and let me go. They were pissed and I loved it! This foolishness has really stressed me out and I know Sy has been worried sick about everything. I think now that things may be quieting down just a bit, there's no better time to get the hell outta dodge….at least for a few days.

****

HHD 1

SYMONE

While I waited for K to come over, I decided to take a nice, hot shower, hoping that would relax my mind and body, but no such luck. I couldn't help wondering who in his circle would dime him out like that. It could be anybody, and that's what was so scary about the whole situation. Hopefully after a good night's sleep, it'll come to me

Just as I was stepping out of the shower, K strolled into the room.

"So they let you go again," I said, shaking my head. "Why do they keep coming and getting you if they ain't got nothing to keep you there?"

"I don't know baby," he wearily replied. "What I DO know is that I'm tired of their shit."

I finished dressing for bed and crawled under the sheets. "Your dinner is in the microwave," I yawned.

He had a confused look on his face. "Why you going to bed already? It's still early."

"I've been running around all day," I told him. "I am completely exhausted."

"Please don't go to sleep just yet. Let me hop in the shower first."

Even in my state of sheer exhaustion, K's naked body had the power to make my pussy quiver. As I listened to the water running in the shower, I felt myself drifting off to sleep. I really must've passed all the way out because the next thing I knew, K's face was between my thighs, doing with his tongue what he does oh so well. If I was exhausted before, I damn sure wasn't now because the way he licked my clit and sucked on my precious pearl, he woke me ALL the way up. It's a good thing my house is the only one tucked away in this nice, small and quiet little cul de sac because if I had neighbors, they would definitely be hearing my very loud screams of pure delight right now.

After that juicy tongue of his made me cum at least 3 times, I simply HAD to mount that big black stallion and ride off into ecstasy. It felt so good, I exploded all over him like I hadn't had sex in months. Then he flipped me over, smacked my ass, grabbed my waist and pulled me back HARD on his manhood. I threw it back at him while he plunged deeper and faster into me. Finally we both came and collapsed across the bed with him still sprawled on top of me. We were so spent neither of us could move, but that didn't last long; 30 minutes later we were right back at it: licking, sticking, bucking and fucking. He even did something he'd never done before: lick my ass! I thought I was going to faint. This had to be the best sex we'd had so far. And as we lay in each arms, drifting off to sleep, K whispered, "I think it's bout time we take another vacation..."

****

Two days later, K and I drove out to a gorgeously quaint little resort called Serenity Springs in LaPorte, In. When we weren't lounging around watching TV and ordering room service, or fucking each other's brains out, we took in the beautiful scenery around the resort, enjoyed a horse and carriage ride and indulged in a couple's massage. It was the most relaxing, romantic 4 days I'd had in a long time. In all honesty, it was too perfect; it was scary perfect. I had a sinking feeling in my gut that had me believing the beauty of this weekend getaway was just a set-up for some hell that was about to break loose.

****

KIM

"Pablo have you been doing some talking to some people?"

"What?" Pablo scoffed, slightly confused.

"I don't know what you're talking about. Sam, tell your bro I'm a good guy."

"I don't know Pablo," Sam said, slowly shaking his head.

"It's been a lot of bullshit going on around here. Somebody DEFINITELY been running they mouth and personally, we think it's you."

"Here, I brought you some of your money," Pablo said, slamming a large leather briefcase on the desk and snapping it open. $200,000 cleaned and washed. The other $50,000 will be ready next week."

I eyeballed the money in the case, looked up at Pablo, then side-eyed Sam. His face said exactly what I was thinking: something real fishy is going on. I shook my head.

"Nah I'm good. You keep that $200,000; I don't know what that's for."

All of a sudden, shit got really real....really quick.

"POLICE! POLICE!"

About 20 cops kicked in the door and barreled their way inside. "Kim Brinkman you are under arrest! Sam Brinkman you are under arrest! You are both being charged with money laundering and a list of other charges."

I calmly put my hands behind my back and gave one final order to my receptionist:

"Erica, call Jane and tell her meet me at the station."

****

HHD 1

SYMONE

"Symone," Jane sighed heavily into the phone. "They got them, and I think it's for good this time. I'm on my way down there now, so I'll call you once I know what's going on. Let Kesh know I'm working on getting Sam a lawyer. Just sit tight...I'll call you in an hour or so."

I was in shock. I kept the phone to my ear for about a minute, thinking I would hear Jane come back on the line and say "SIKE!" But when she didn't, I quickly swallowed to stop the tears from coming and began to pray. When I told Kesh, she immediately started bawling.

"Why does shit like this always happen to me?" she wailed, burying her face in her hands. "He just proposed to me last night Sy."

She pulled the ring out of her bag and showed me; a gorgeous 2 carat chocolate diamond ring. "It's one size too small; we were supposed to go get it resized today," she whimpered.

I grabbed her. hugging her close while we both just sat there for a few minutes, crying and rocking each other. Finally, I pulled away from her and wiped her face.

"Congratulations bitch, we both getting married. Now let's go get that ring resized. Ain't like either of us got shit else to do right now."

****

As we pulled back into my driveway, Jane pulled in right behind me. She ushered me into the living room and gave me the rundown as I poured each of us a glass of wine.

"Their bond hearing is tomorrow. I'm not sure if he wants to be bailed out or not, but he said he would let me know tomorrow. He said there's a safe in one of your guest bedrooms; the code is the date of your engagement. He also made it very clear that he does NOT want you to come to court because he doesn't want them messing with you and your business. I will call you tomorrow to let you know what he wants to do."

"Ok, thanks sis. We truly appreciate everything you're doing to help us. Let me know what your fees are and I'll pay you tomorrow."

Jane grabbed both my hands and squeezed.

"Sy, we have far more pressing matters right now. We'll deal with all that later."

****

Ain't this some shit? I didn't even know he put a safe in here. When the hell did that happen? Once I found it, under the damn bed of all places, it took me a few tries but I finally got it open. There was more money in there than I'd ever seen in my entire life, and it made me nervous. As I eyeballed the stacks, terrified of touching them, I spotted the letter:

> **Bae,**
>
> **First, I'm sorry that we're even in this situation, but the man caught up with me before I could get out. I have a snitch in my circle. I never had this problem when I was dealing with Keo and Paul but I think it's that fool Pablo that Sam brought in. I need you to take all the money in the safe and put it in a safe deposit box. It should be 3 million. Have you sister keep money on my books; Kesh will**

take care of Sam's books. This is for you to do what you please. I'm trusting you with everything I got. I also need you to go see Paul and Keo. A guy named Mike will call the phone I left in this safe; just tell him your name is Bottom Bitch, or BB. They'll know exactly who you are. You should only have to deal with them two, maybe three times. I also need you to do my mom's company's payroll, then hire an accountant for her please. I know this a lot I'm asking of you, but trust and believe you will have anything you want as soon as this is all over. I love you with everything in me. Don't sell my house and keep up with the shops. They both have managers; just do the drops. There is a power of attorney to all my stuff til I am released. Use if it need be. If not, leave it as is. I guess either Kesh or Momma B will watch over his clothing store. I know Jane will keep you updated.

Love Always,

K

****

HHD 1

It felt like today was never going to come. I tossed and turned all night, unable to shut my brain off. All I could do was think about everything that had just been placed on my shoulders. K is my man, so without question I'm going to do whatever he needs me to do; the suddenness of it all is just very overwhelming.

Jane finally got to my house, I thought I was on the verge of a breakdown. She explained that K's bond was $500,000; meaning, it'll take $50,000 to get him out. However, he prefers not to be bonded out because he knows not only will HE continue to be followed, now that they definitely know who I am, they'll be following me too. So he'd rather sit this out. He found out his other shop was raided last night as well, so he instructed the managers, Al and Slim, to call me today. Jane also finally confirmed his charges: two counts of money laundering and a number of drug charges, which she said they have no evidence of, so more than likely, those charges will be dropped.

My mind was swirling with all the info she was dropping on me, but it made me even more determined to hold my man down. *I gotta find who the snitch is in his circle, and when I do, he's gonna wish he never had a mouth to fuckin' open...*

****

As soon as Jane left, "Bottom Bitch" got straight to work, doing everything K instructed "her" to in his letter:

First, I called Keo and told him to meet me in 2 hours on West Kilbourn. Then I called Mike and told him to meet me the following evening in the CitiTrends parking lot on 119th and Halstead. I called Paul next; unfortunately, he didn't answer, so I stressed the urgency of his return call on his voice mail. This was some crazy ass shit. I actually called all three of these guys on a separate cell phone.

Once I hung up from calling Paul, there was a knock on my door; it was Mel. Damn was I glad to see her. I knew she had connections all over the city, so I asked her to find out any info she could on the undercover officer handling K's case, as well as the presiding Judge. Mel is the best in the biz, so I knew a number of police, attorneys and judges were frequent clients of her services. I paid her $5,000 up front and promised her another $5,000 once she presented me with the info I needed.

"I know you know how to work it," I said, licking my lips. "Now how bout you come work me, cuz I sure need it right now."

****

Later that evening, I met Keo at Club Allure, HIS club. You never know what people are into these days.

"Let's go in the back office," he said, leading the way.

"Damn it's a lot of security in here," I said, eyeballing a gigantic bodyguard who heavily favored the actor Tiny Lister.

"We need all of this security to protect our money. No need to pat her down," he told 'Tiny Lister.' "If K sent her, I know she good."

At this point, all I could think is *Damn, K got clout like this?*

"So what you got for me?" Keo asked as he leaned back in his plush white leather chair and lit a Cuban.

"Damn..right down to business huh," I chuckled. "I like that."

Keo placed the shiny, black leather briefcase atop his glass desk and snapped it open. "I got $90,000, plus my $10,000 right here, all washed and cleaned."

I looked over the stacks in the case while he blew three perfect rings of smoke into the air.

"Ok, this is good. I will see you in two days. This the final shipment."

I breathed a huge sigh of relief and smiled. My baby finally getting out the game. *When all this is over, he owes me a HUGE vacation, cuz lawd knows I'mma need it.*

****

The next day, I went to the bank and opened an account with a safe deposit attached to it. I deposited half of the rest of the money into the account and secured the remainder in the safe deposit. Next I headed over to check on Momma B and handle some of my own affairs. I also called Kesh to update her on everything. I know she's having a rough time over there but she sounded like she was trying to keep it together. I filled her in on everything I knew, told her to come see me tomorrow so we could console each other, and headed over to the other shop.

HHD 1

SYMONE

I've gotten a lot done in the 4 months that K has been away. I got him out the game, all his money is now clean and I've finally got it put up for safe keeping. Now Keo is talking about a sit down with me and some of the bosses. I wish I could run this past K to see what he thinks about it. I'll text Jane and have her get the message to him. As I completed the text, it suddenly dawned on me that I hadn't heard from Mel in a minute.

> *Me: "Come see me ASAP"*
> *Mel: "Ok I got something for you too."*
> *Me: "Is it   some freaky shit?"*
> *Mel: "That too."*
> *Me: "Yes, I'm long overdue. It's been awhile. You've been neglecting me."*
> *Mel: "Give me 45 mins"*
> *Me: "OK."*

Running back and forth between the boutiques all day reminded me that I really hadn't eaten, so I strolled happily into the kitchen to begin dinner:

shrimp and grits. Dinner was just about done when there was a knock at the door. My lips immediately spread into a huge smile because I knew exactly who it was.

"What up boo, where you been hiding?" I grinned as I opened the door.

She gave me a wink and a smile and said, "I've been busy working that number for you."

We made our way to the kitchen and I started taking up our food. I gave her a plate and a glass of wine, grabbed my food and glass and we went and got comfortable on the couch. Once we settled in, she handed me a folder. In the folder was the undercover cop info, district attorney and judge. My girl! I knew she could do it! I'm going to make sure she gets paid WELL for this.....financially and in "other" ways.

****

KIM

"Jane what's going on with all these continuances?" I asked, throwing my hands up exasperatedly.

"They've been slow giving me all the evidence they have against you," Jane explained. "I think they don't have a case as strong as they initially thought. I'll file a motion in the morning. Until then…we're sitting ducks."

"Ok that's cool. In the meantime, how's my baby?"

"She's good…staying strong."

I smiled wide. "Yeah the fellas and my mom tell me she's staying on top of all the business. I've got to think of a good gift after all this."

"Oh! Here are a few letters from her," she said, digging in her purse and handing them to me.

"Annnnd on ANOTHER note…she found out that Sam has been doing business with Officer Erik/Pablo for a while before he brought him to your attention."

I jerked my head up from the letters.

"Oh really?! How long this shit been going on?"

"Maybe like a year or two," she replied. "My friend has got all of Sam's case stuff but they can't try him until they're done with you. So as it stands right now, he's only being charged with accessory."

"So to be clear…"

I said pointedly, sitting up in my seat, "what you're saying is that my brother has been dirty dealing with this mutha-fucka behind my damn back? What kind of business have they been doing?"

Jane shrugged. "I don't know but don't worry about it. I WILL find out. I truly believe he was a dirty cop K. I'm working on that to see if that was part of his cover or was he really dirty. Maybe Sam knows something we don't."

I gave a Jane a real evil smile.

"Oh he better know something, and I need you to come see me as soon as you find out. And if he IS a dirty ass cop, I'll definitely be out sooner than we think."

****

HHD 1

SYMONE

I grabbed me a glass of wine, sat on the couch and started reading through all the info that Mel gave me:

Officer Erik Ridge a.k.a. "Pablo"
Married to Elliana Ridge
Two children: twin girls named Rayne and Elise.

Judge Sandra Lipinski.
Divorced
Three children: two in college; one a lawyer.

The right people can find out anything about you I see. Now let me look at the States attorney file. They say she's a real cocky bitch.

Sara Maxim
No kids (Good! That means no one will miss her ass.)
Only child
Parents: Edith and Samuel Maxim, owners of The Lucky Lady magazine corporation.

She's a spoiled brat....that's her problem. I got a solution for all this. She lives in a condo on Hollywood Blvd. I wonder if there's an opening in her building? Hmmmm…think I'll call first thing in the morning and see. Time to put this plan in motion.

****

Jane and I met up for lunch the next day at Café Ole. I was already there when she arrived so I waved her over to our table.

"What up sis? I already ordered for us, so let's get on down to bid'ness," I said, rubbing my hands together and scooting up in my chair.

"Ok, so you know I do K's mom's books for her business right? Well Sam has been doing some shady side shit with that cop and it's been with his mom's business. He definitely got money put up somewhere. And I swear I can't seem to put my finger on it, but that cop knows. That's why since they've been locked up, they've been to her business a few times looking for paperwork. The sad part is I don't think Kim knows."

"Oh honey, I told him last week that Sam and that cop been doing some side business," Jane said, sipping on her Arnold Palmer. "I just didn't realize it was through his moms business. Honestly, I think Sam got something on that cop; that's why they ain't coming for him as hard as they are K."

I sucked my teeth. "I wonder if that's why Sam ain't speaking up or is HE on some sneaky shit too."

"Maybe he's thinking if he snitch on the cop that'll open doors for them to charge him with some extra stuff," Jane suggested. "I've got an investigator working on some things anyway so I'll tell him to look into it. Can you get me copies of the paperwork in Sam's office? I need to look it over with a fine toothed comb."

"No prob. I gotta do payroll tomorrow anyway so I'll call you then."

The waiter brought our entrees and we spent the next 5 minutes adding our condiments and taking very hungry bites of our food.

In between bites, my phone rang.

"Hello?"

"Hello, may I speak to Symone please?" the voice on the other end requested.

"This is she," I confirmed. Trying to catch her voice.

"Hi Symone, this is Angel. I'm returning your call regarding the condo I have available."

GAME TIME!

"Yes hi," I said, smiling wider than I actually meant to. She told me her 2:30 appointment had cancelled and if I was available at that time, she could show it to me then. I excitedly told her yes and that I'd see her in an hour.

As soon as I hung up, I waved the waiter over and asked him for a to-go box and the check. Jane was still eating and looked at me like "what the hell?"

"I have some serious business to tend to Sis so I gotta go. I promise I'll fill you in later." I left the money for our lunches on the table, kissed her on the cheek and hauled ass, leaving her with her mouth still gaped open.

****

When I stepped off the elevator on the top floor of the Lakeview Apartment building, I came face-to-face with this 5ft2in, 187lbs beauty with a 38 D chest, nice thick hips and some juicy ass lips. GotDAMN she was sexy!

"Hello, Symone. I'm Angel," she smiled, holding out her hand for us to shake. Damn! Even her hands are sexy. *Come on back Sy.....this ain't what you here for!*

"Hello Angel," I smiled back. "Glad I was able to make it. I'm very excited to see the apartment."

"Well then let me walk you through then," she said, unlocking the door and leading the way inside. We walked down 3 steps into a living room damn near the size of a football field and my feet sank deep into the beautiful beige plush carpeting. From there, she led me to the master bedroom, which included a step down Jacuzzi, his-and-her sinks, a toilet, walk-in shower and a walk-in closet. The bedroom also boasted an absolutely gorgeous view of downtown Chicago. The second bedroom was just as huge as the master. Angel told me the last tenant used it as an office/extra storage space.

Next, she showed me the full guest bathroom and kitchen equipped with stainless steel everything, including the dishwasher and microwave. She also made sure to walk me back into the living room so I could take in the amazing view of the skyline, which is even more beautiful at night when it's lit up.

"Now what did you say you did for a living?" Angel asked me.

I was right on cue with an answer.

"I own my own catering business. So what are the neighbors like?"

She grinned slow and wide.

"Oh they're good people. One is an attorney, the other is a clothes designer and the other is an accountant. Hopefully we can add you to the bunch. So does this mean you're interested in the condo then?"

"Yes, I love it," I grinned back. "How much is it to move in?"

"Well it's $1,500 a month rent. So you'll need your first month, plus last month and security."

"So $4,500 to move in then?" I smiled as I began filling out the cashier's check.

She couldn't even hide how impressed she was.

"Oh well alright Miss Thang," she laughed. "Let's head downstairs to my place so we can get this paperwork knocked out then."

When I walked inside her apartment, I had to stop myself from sounding like a damn groupie. Her shit was laid out, like she must have bought out the whole IKEA store. I felt my mouth hanging open so I quickly closed it and said, "My...you have a gorgeous place here."

"Thank you so much," she replied.

"I love to shop and shopping for things to decorate my place is one of my fave past times."

She disappeared to the back of her apartment and returned with a stack of papers, which she handed to me.

"Here's the paperwork I need you to fill out as well as your receipt, your keys to the door and the pool and the code to the entrance gate. You'll need to have the utilities in your name by Monday. Sign here and here and I will make you a copy of your lease. The condo comes with two parking spots and we also have a get together once a week. As a matter fact, there's one tonight. Would you like to join us?"

I honestly didn't feel like being bothered, but I had to remind myself why I was here, so I just said

"Yes, sure where's it going to be?"

Rubbing her fingers thru her hair, she said

"Right here at 7:00."

I caught her staring at me again, and since she noticed that I'd caught her, she just came out with it.

"Symone I don't mean to come off unprofessional or anything, but has anyone ever told you that you are fine as hell?"

Though taken slightly aback, I didn't show it; I just smiled.

"Yes, but…definitely not the way you put it. You're sexy your damn self." She got up out her chair and started towards the kitchen.

She looked back at me and said,

"Oh hell yeah, you're really going to fit in well here. The attorney likes women too. Would you like something to drink?" she offered.

"Yeah sure," I accepted. As she sashayed into the kitchen, I couldn't stop myself from ogling her thick ass as it swished and wobbled from left to right. I imagined myself massaging each luscious cheek as I buried my face in her…

"I have Ciroc and cranberry juice is that ok?" she asked, interrupting my fantasy.

"Yeah that's fine," I said, nodding my head. She came out the kitchen with both drinks in hand, and as she handed me mine, she made sure to put those double D's of hers in my face.

"Yeeeeaaah…." she purred, licking those juicy lips of hers. "You are super sexy."

My pussy immediately quivered, so in an effort to ignore the inevitable, I took 2 giant swigs of my drink and said,

"Damn Angel you should be a bartender; this drink is delish."

Before I could put the glass back to my lips, she took it out of my hand and began to kiss me. I instantly got wet. She grabbed my hand and guided me to her bedroom, and she lay across the bed, I kept telling myself that I wasn't here for this….that I needed to stay focused. But all that went clean out the window when Angel mushed her face deep inside my pussy.

****

She told me she hadn't creamed like that in years. I told her I was happy to oblige her. While I showered, she freshened my drink. Something in me was telling me she had a motive, but at the same time, I was coming up with my own plan to turn her and that attorney against each other. When I opened my eyes from my thoughts, she'd climbed into the shower and began to wash my back. *Thank God I don't have any plans today,* I laughed to myself. She started telling me about all the other tenants, especially the attorney. Damn…this is easier than I thought it would be.

"So have you slept with the attorney?" I asked.

"Oh hell yeah," she said.

"I made sure I tested those waters. She's good, but you're better. I can set something up for all three of us if you want me too," she anxiously suggested.

I'm glad I still had my back turned to her because the annoyed look I had on my face definitely would've given me away. Instead I just laughed and said, "Oh hell nawl! I can't be smashing two women in the same building; that shit will cause all kindsa trouble."

HHD 1

After going at it a couple more times, her freaky ass finally went to sleep, so I sneaked out and went back upstairs to MY place. I immediately called a locksmith to come out and change the locks to the door and the code to the safe that was already in the apartment. Then I ran out to my car and grabbed my overnight bag that I always keep on hand. Determined to relax for a little while, I ordered me a pizza and jumped in the shower. Just as I was stepping out of the shower, my phone rang….it was Jane.

She told me that she'd just returned from seeing Kim and that he gave her a few letters to give me. She also told him what I'd found out and he wanted me to try to find out how Sam had been doing business with "Pablo." She said she'd been waiting on Sam's lawyer to call her back but she still hadn't. She thinks his attorney is trying to get his case tossed out and if it does, then undoubtedly Kim's will too. Lastly, she let me know that she'd filed a motion earlier today making everyone turn over any and all evidence to her.

"Sam don't know I do payroll," I told Jane, "so his ass think he getting away smooth. He has no idea I'm an accountant; he just think I got businesses. So if he trying to snake K, I'll damn sure find it."

Jane sighed wearily. "I'm not sure Sis, but it sure looks that way. Just promise me you won't tell Kesh til we find out for sure."

I promised her I wouldn't. Kesh was getting stronger every day as she continued on with her daily affairs. This news right here...would fuck her all up.

****

After I ate my pizza, I stretched out across my bed, hoping I could at least grab me a couple hours sleep before this little shindig started. I swear I'd just sunk into a deep sleep when my damn phone rang. I was able to ignore it the first time but whoever was calling was determined to get me to pick up.

"Hello?" I snapped, not even trying to hide the irritation in my voice.

HHD 1

"Awwww I didn't mean to wake you…"

Angel's voice cooed on the other end. "The meet up is about to get under way and I just wanted to make sure you were still coming. Everybody's anxious to meet their new neighbor."

Damn I don't feel like this shit tonight.

"Oh I'm excited to meet them too," I lied.

"I just didn't realize how tired I was. Give me 30 minutes and I'll be down."

"Okie dokie! See ya then!" she sang into the phone as she hung up.

I got up and started getting dressed. It was time to really put this master plan in motion. I slid into my black mini dress by Sheem'a, the one that perfectly hugs every single curve on my body like a second skin, along with my leopard print Christian Louboutin shoe boots. My ponytail was flawless and the only makeup I chose to wear was some eyeliner, mascara and gloss on my lips. Shit….now I truly understand the meaning behind Tweet's song because looking in this mirror is making me want to touch my damn self. Oh yes…this was going to be a VERY interesting night indeed. Time to make these hoes fight over me.

HHD 1

"Hey Symone," Angel gushed as she flung open the door.

"Come on in and meet everyone! This is Sara.....Aj.....Jasmine.....and Sherry. Everyone this is Symone, our new neighbor."

We all said our "hello's" and "nice to meet you's," trying to feel each other out in the process.

"So can I get you to drink?" she asked me. "I got Ciroc, Hennessey, Patron and Moscato.

"I'll take the same thing you gave me earlier. That was yummy," I said, emphasizing the word "yummy." I got a side eye from the Sara chick, and she immediately walked over to me.

"So Symone, how do you like it here so far?" she asked.

I smiled. "It's ok. I like it."

"I considered getting the penthouse but that's too much room for me," she said, almost sounding braggy.

"So what do you do for a living?"

I took a long sip of my drink before responding.

"I own a catering business. How about you Sara?"

"I'm a prosecutor for the State's Attorney's office," she replied proudly.

I pretended to be impressed.

"Oh really now? Well I know who to call if I get in trouble," I laughed. "How about you AJ? What do you do?"

"I'm a designer for Sheem'a. As a matter fact, I've been scoping your body out since you walked in and I've got a few fabulous pieces that will look great on you."

I got excited about that. "Ooooo yeeesssss! That's my absolute FAVE designer! Just let me know when and I'm there! What about you Jasmine and Sherry?"

"I'm an accountant," Jasmine replied. "And Sherry here is a newspaper editor for Southtown." I was bored out of my mind, but I continued with the pleasantries, thinking to myself *I'm outta here in the next hour.*

HHD 1

As the night wore on, we all continued talking and getting to know each other, eventually ending up in the pool together. I noticed that Sara and Angel were both vying for my attention HARD. Whenever I gravitated towards either one of and "clung" for too long, the other made sure to find a reason to turn my attention away. I also started noticing how sexy Jasmine was, so I made a point of getting next to her as much as possible too, which pissed them both off. It was all I could do not to laugh out loud. Jealously was in full effect and I loved it! *I'mma have these bitches burning the complex down by the time I'm done with them.*

Finally this bullshit was coming to a close for the evening and I couldn't have been more relieved. We all said good night and headed to our respective apartments, promising to make plans to all get together again soon, as well as making individual plans with each other. As soon as I got home, I immediately jumped in the shower. The pool felt great, but now all that chlorine had my body itching. Fast as I stepped my big toe in the shower, somebody knocked at the damn door. I shook my head and laughed. *I'll bet I know who this is.* I wrapped myself in a towel and went to the door.

"Who is it?" I asked, as if I didn't already know.

"It's Sara," she whispered. *Of course it is*, I said to myself. I knew she was coming so I didn't even bother locking the door.

"Come on in, it's open."

"Oh…I see your condo came fully furnished like mine," she mentioned as she followed me back to the bathroom.

She know damn well she don't care about this condo. "Yup it sure did," I replied.

She stepped into the shower with me and started washing my back and kissing me on my neck and shoulders. I turned around and kissed her, then she went straight down and started to giving me some head. I threw my head back and started riding her face. Damn she was a pro at this shit. My mind went to K. I wish this was him instead of any of these females. Once the water got cold, we got out and moved to the couch, where she went back to eating me out and fingering my ass at the same time. I begin to suck on my own nipples and I could feel my juices flowing, but I was waiting for that big orgasm.

"Lick my ass and finger my pussy," I moaned. She immediately did what I requested, eating my ass as if it was her last supper and massaging my pearl like an expert. Oh shit....this was feeling so good I started calling out K's name. I suggested we go to her condo so we could play with some of her toys. She was game for that. I was about to have her sprung. That was one of my goals....to fuck her mind all the way up.

****

I slept til about 10 the next morning. All that fucking wore me slap the hell out. I dragged myself out of bed, showered and threw on some baggy shorts and a t-shirt. I headed to Mom Duke's house to pick up the letters that Jane had for me but I didn't stay long. It's her Gin and tea day with the ladies and I wasn't in the mood for their brand of "turn up" today. She loves those women. They do more cussing than the law allow, especially Kesh and Lisa's moms. I texted Jane, praying she was home so I wouldn't have to go inside.

Me: Hey I'm on the way to the house now to pick up the letters. You home?

J: Nope. Went into the office to get some work done. You know it's Tea Day and I can't get shit done with them cackling like a bunch of old hens.

Me: Damn! I was trying NOT to have to go inside.

J: They gone talk yo ass to death lol.

Me: Ha ha. Where the letters at?

J: On your bed, where I always leave them

Me: Sigh....ok. I'm going in. Pray for me.

J: Lol

****

It took me almost an hour to separate myself from them damn ladies but I finally made it back to the comfort of my REAL home. I didn't feel like being anywhere near that condo while I engrossed myself in these letters from my man. I grabbed a bottle of Duplin off the rack, got me a glass out the cabinet and snuggled into my couch pillows.

Dear Wife,

Thanks for taking care of my mom first and foremost. She talks about you the whole time when I call her. She says if we weren't already together she'd marry you herself lol. I had to tell her she was too late because I already "put a ring on it." She says we need kids asap. I personally can't wait. I know you'll be a fantastic mother to and for our children.

I got permission to write Sam. He wrote back...said he was cool. That's it. He said he ready to go home and get married. Telling me shit I already know basically and none of what I really need to know. But it's all good though. This shit definitely ain't over.

About the Keo situation: go see him. I grew up with Keo and Paul. They good people. I can bet my last $ they meeting about some money. If they want an answer right away, just use your own judgment. I trust you. We should be done with Mike also. How are the shops? The fellas say you treating them cool. They came to see me the other day.

I miss the taste of that monkey and the feel of that pussy. I bet Mel been taking good care of that for me. She going to be mad when I get out cause we are going to be M.I.A for a while and plus you going to be too sore to let anyone else touch that. I got a lot of pinned up nut and stress in this dick. I need to explode asap. I just need you to cream down my throat. I need to smack that ass to. I miss cooking for you. I miss cuddling with you. Shit...I miss Blue too lol.

Finally, yet most importantly, I need you to take 100G's and go find us a house. We need to move in together and just rent our places out. Then do your thang and decorate. My only request is a man cave where I can have the fellas over. Let me know what area you looking in. I prefer a 4br/2.5 or 3ba. Spot with a nice, big backyard for our future kids. What you think? I can't wait to hear back from you. I love you baby.

Your Husband.

I felt so warm inside after I finished his letter. I must've read it at least 5 times, smiling bigger each time. I jumped on the phone and called Keo. He told me to be at his crib by 3pm the next day. Once that was taken care of, I realized it was time to get some clothes moved into that condo because I just know those nosy heffas are watching me. I decided to text Sara and invite her along, mainly to start digging her for some info, but also because I knew it would piss Angel off. She was only too happy to join me and told me she had THE perfect spot for us to shop: Boutique So Chic downtown. I told her to meet me in an hour.

****

After fighting all that traffic I finally made it.

"Heyyy Sara," I said giving her a hug when I walked in. "Let's see what this shop has. I'm trusting you because I've never been here before."

"Girl you will love it. I promise. I do the majority of my shopping here. So how did your lunch catering go?"

I almost said what lunch catering, then I remembered that's what I told her to get away from her this morning. "Oh it went great. Thanks for asking. How was your day?"

She took a deep breath and exhaled hard. I could tell she needed to get something off her chest. "It was ok for the most part. I just can't wait to get one of my cases over with."

I was hoping she was talking about K's case. "Really? How come?"

Her frustration took over. "It's because this guy is cocky....as if he just KNOWS that we don't have enough against him to keep him in jail for more than six months. All the evidence we DID have is falling apart. So I keep having to continue the case until we build some more evidence."

My heart was going a million miles a minute but I played it cool.

"Oh wow. Well I sure hope you get him. What did he do, if you don't mind me asking?

She looked around the store and moved closer to me. "He and his brother are charged with money laundering. They got businesses and homes and all types a shit as a result of this but most of it isn't even in their names and we have no idea how to seize any of it because we don't know whose names to search. It's fucking frustrating.

HHD 1

She started whipping angrily through the rack of clothes in front of us. "But trust and believe....we ARE gonna nail these mutha-fuckas to the wall."

I side-eyed her. It was all I could do not to hang her little ass off one of these clothes racks. "Oh wow! Yeah he AND his damn brother need to be locked up," I said trying to remain calm. On the inside though, I was thinking *Bitch...you really have no idea who the fuck you playin' with right now...*

HHD 1

SYMONE

As I pulled into the winding driveway and coasted up to the address that was provided to me, my mouth dropped open. The outside structure of this home was absolutely opulent, so I knew the inside couldn't be any less amazing. It was nestled in the Park Forest subdivision and sat way back "in the cut;" basically, you definitely could NOT see it from the street. It sat on at least 3 acres of land and included security guards stationed at every corner of the house.

Once I reached the front door, I buzzed the outside intercom and was greeted by a woman's strong Russian accent. I told her who I was and the door was immediately opened. The woman, who I assumed was Mr. Green's assistant, welcomed me inside and told me he was expecting me. She leads me through this maze of a house up to a set of two huge French doors and presses another intercom on the wall. "Miss BB is here," she said, and once again, the doors were immediately opened.

Inside were six guys sitting at a conference table. I strutted in with all the confidence of a peacock and everyone stood up. Paul guided to me an empty seat next to the head of the table and pulled it out for me to sit. Only when my bottom connected with the plush leather cushion did the men retake their seats. I was very impressed at the level of respect they exuded, yet I still had no idea why my presence was even requested.

Finally I just asked. "So why am I here fellas?"

"You do know all of us, right?" Paul asked.

"Yes I do," I replied. "I just didn't realize that all of you knew each other. I thought only you and Paul knew each other because you and Kim grew up together. He told me y'all were in the game when you were shorties. When he got locked up, you two held him down."

"You know a lot I see," Keo smirked.

"Noooooo....I just know enough to know who I'm messing with," I corrected.

"So does Kim know that you're here?" Paul asked.

"What does that matter?" I snapped.

"You asked me to be here, so I'm here. And again I ask: why AM I here?"

Mike roared with laughter. "Damn she feisty Keo! I like that!"

Keo checked him quick. "Watch yourself Mike; that's my boy's lady. Don't get no ideas; people die over shit like that."

Mike threw up his hands in surrender.

"Man it ain't even like that. I just mean she bout her shit and ain't taking no prisoners...that's all."

Keo smiled and said, "True. Wrong metaphor, but I catch what you're saying."

Mike shook his head in frustration. "Damn y'all know what I meant."

"It's ok Mike," Paul said, trying to diffuse the situation. "I know what you saying bro."

I almost giggled out loud. I was like, *damn...so I have a little bit of clout up in this bitch huh?* I felt rather boss diva'ish at that moment, so I regained control of the room and said,

"Sooooo...ONCE AGAIN, for the last damn time before I get up and walk out of here....WHY AM I HERE?"

"Damn BB calm down," Keo laughed. "Alright, alright let's get down to business here. So, Mike is the man who brings the coke in. Paul and I wash the money at our clubs, and Les and AB help us at our other clubs so it goes faster and smoother. The problem is, we don't know who sells the coke and brings back the money that you bring us to wash. So YOU hold a piece of the puzzle that we don't have. Also, Mike wants out the game and he has one big shipment that he needs to get off and send the man back his money. Then we will all be free and clear."

"OK, this is all fine and dandy but that's not telling me why I'M here," I reiterated.

Paul looked around the table at his men, then took a very deep breath. "We need the middleman, or men."

I kept my face stern. "Why y'all can't get your own hustlers? You six are very important people and I'm quite sure you have connects somewhere."

"We don't want to start fresh," he explained. "We want someone who's already been handling the merchandise."

I was curious to know how I would benefit from this, so I sat up bone-straight in my chair, clasped my hands on the table and quietly asked, "So IF I'm down, then what do I get out this deal?"

Keo blinked. "What exactly do you want?"

I sat back in my seat and said, "Make me an offer. And precisely when is all this is due to take place?"

"The better question is…..do you have to ask Kim?" Mike asked.

"Ha-ha what's my name?" I quipped with a smirk. "Say it with me now…BB! That means while the DICK is away the PUSSY shall play."

Mike laughed. "So I'll take that as a NO."

"We're looking at it to happen ASAP," Paul spoke up.

I cut straight back to the chase.

"Excuse me? No one is telling me what MY percentage of this deal will be. Matter fact, tell me how much they need to move and I will tell you what I expect and we can negotiate from there."

"Mike how much is it?" Keo asked.

"Sixty kilos Keo."

I started to do the math in my head. Then I calmly asked, "So before I say what I want, what are the REST of you are getting out this deal? Is it the normal 10% or is it more? How much do you owe the man off sixty keys? I know you will bring back around 1.5 if he charging you 25 per key. So how much do we in this room have to work with? Or should I keep estimating?"

"He gets 60% clean money off top; if it's dirty, he wants 70%."

I immediately clicked on the mental calculator in my brain. "So that leaves $600,000 for us to split, which, in essence, really only means $450,000 for us to split because you got to pay the people to move it. Paul and Keo will get 15% of this run, which means $136,000 goes to them off top to split, which TECHNICALLY only leaves $314,000. Is there anyone else we got to pay?"

"Les and AB get $10,000 each," Keo replied.

"So then the ACTUAL final total left is $294,000." I looked around the table at them and asked, "So then what the hell are you offering me?"

"Damn BB! What the fuck are you? An accountant?" Paul howled.

I laughed and said, "Nah, I'm just great at math."

"We can offer you $50,000," Mike said.

My attitude quickly shifted. "The fuck I look like?" I spat, snapping my neck in his direction. "I don't even make phone calls for $50,000. Meeting adjourned. I'm out," I said, standing up as I chucked them the deuces.

"Wait!" Paul jumped up. "Tell us what you want."

"$110,000," I replied without even so much as batting an eyelash.

"What??!" Mike yelled. "Wait....no that's too damn much!"

I smiled and slowly repeated, "Like I said...make me an offer."

Keo hung his head in deep thought. "How about $100,000?"

I gave him a grin wider and toothier than a Cheshire cat.

"I'll take it, but I would have accepted $94,000. So exactly when will this shipment be in?"

"From our understanding, it'll be here tonight," Paul replied.

"Tonight?" I released a heavy sigh. "Damn...I guess I need to make moves today, huh? Well, let me get out of here. Keo, I'll call you in an hour or two."

As I was leaving, I heard Mike saying, "Yoooo! THAT lady there got her shit together! Kim got him a real smart chick on his hands. She gon' make sure he set for life when he gets out. "

HHD 1

****

As soon as I got back in my car, I called Marv. I told him I had 60 keys for him plus an extra $130K for his trouble. Of course he got REAL excited because this meant more money for him in the end. *He's so damn desperate with it, he didn't even care that the shit was coming to him dirty,* which I thought was really dumb. The dealer is supposed to make money off what they sell. Why give them the money up front? Oh well…whatever. I told him I'd call him later with the location for us to meet and hung up.

Next, I texted Sara to see if Angel was still mad about walking in on us the other day:

Me: "Hey boo what's up?"

Sara: "Nothing much. Working on this case."

Me: "You a hard worker."

Sara: "Yes I am lol. I go on vacation next week and I'm flying out to New York to buy me a few things. I deserve it. Would you like to come?"

HHD 1

Me: "Ummm...sure! Will let my worker know she needs to cover a breakfast for me. When do we leave?"

Sara: "In a few days."

Me:" OK. Tmr we have drinks at my house. Is Angel bk speaking to us? Is she mad or nah? kmsl"

Sara: "I really dnt knw. She will get over it tho. So what are we having at your hse?"

Me: "Drinks, taco salad, pizza and playing Uno or Phase 10"

Sara: "Cool, do you need me to bring anything?"

Me: "Just your sexy self."

Sara: "Lol I can do that. Wyd tonight?"

Me: "Nothing. Watching a movie and eating a Gyro."

Sara: "Can I come over?"

Me: "Sure. Angel going to be extra mad lol."

HHD 1

Sara: "Fk her. Grab me one too. I'll be there by six".

Me: "k TTYL"

****

As soon as Sara walked inside, she shoved a letter in my hand.

"Look what was sticking in my office door as I was leaving…"

Dear Sara,

I see you and your "lady friend" have been getting awful close. I wonder do your parents know that their only baby girl is GAY. Or if your office staff know. Let's see what they'll think of you in the corporate world then. They'll all be talking about you then. You'll never know who I am because your dumb blond ass has sent so many people to jail, a lot of people hate you. Don't ask how I got in the building; you'll never find out. I will hurt you and all your neighbors. Enjoy the rest of your week and weekend.

Angry Defendant

"Damn," I sighed, shaking my head. "Who do you think sent this? You think it's Angel trying to be funny? Or maybe an ex?"

"I don't know what to think," Sara said wearily.

"The only time we've ever been together was dinner and shopping. It's strange that Angel's not home. She's usually always there."

"Did you call her and see if she answers?" I asked.

"No I didn't because I know she's behind all this," Sara huffed.

"But what if she's not?" I asked.

"Then I don't know who it is," Sara spat, throwing up her hands.

"I've literally put away over 200 people in my career so far so it could be anybody. I know one damn thing though...THIS ain't what he or she wants! I will shoot a bitch dead and bury they ass the same day!"

I giggled nervously. "Calm down hon. Just keep trying to get in touch with her."

"I got keys to her place," Sara said. "If she still hasn't answered by the time I leave here, I'll swing by her apartment on my way home."

****

After hanging at my house for a few hours, as well as numerous unsuccessful attempts at trying to reach Angel, we made our way over to her place. When we walked in, her apartment was completely dark except for her hallway light.

"Angel?" I called out. "Are you in here?" I looked back at Sara and her face held the same question that neither of us had an answer for: where the hell could she possibly be?

I asked Sara if she had any family nearby and she said from her understanding, she only has one sister who lives in Philly. Their parents were killed when they were in New York for business during

9/11; that's how she gained ownership of the apartment building she lives in. Her sister is an investment banker who's married to one of them "uppity type Negros" who thinks he's white. I was growing more worried by the minute, but I suggested we give her a day or two to pop back up and if she didn't, we should call the police. Sara also said if all else fails, we could call her sister. Hopefully she knew where she was.

After we left Angel's apartment, we went over to chill out at Sara's house. To take our minds off worrying about Angel, I told her to tell me everything there was to know about Sara. She told me she was an only child and her parents own Lucky Magazine, one of the most popular news and entertainment magazines in the country. She worked hard to put herself through law school on her own because she wanted to be able to look back and say that she accomplished it without Mommy's influence or Daddy's money. She endured a lot of bullshit in college; the guys assumed because she was a gorgeous, blue-eyed blonde that she was nothing more than an airhead and a party girl, and all the girls simply thought she was a ho sleeping with everybody's man. Well, she shut all the naysayers up when she graduated, with honors, from Yale's School of Law and worked her up to becoming state's attorney.

"Well I am an only child. My parents own Lucky magazine. I love to shop. I worked hard to get thru law school and to become state's attorney...' She absolutely loves her job, but hates the stress that comes along with it. She went on to say that her parents have been hounding her to retire and take over the magazine; they've only given her a year to consider it.

"Which way are you leaning?" I asked.

She rubbed her head. "I'm not sure. I do know the ins and outs of the company, but I absolutely love being in the courtroom."

"Ok…so run the magazine on the side and continue to be an attorney," I suggested.

She smiled at me. "That's a great idea. I seriously never thought of that. But I love here in Chi-town though; they're in LA."

"Simple...just run it from here," I explained. "Find you someone who's already THERE to manage the office duties, that way you can stay HERE."

I could tell she was deep in thought about what I'd just presented her.

"Hmmm... definitely food for thought," she grinned.

****

After making the exchange with Marv and swinging by the shops to check on the fellas, Sara and I were FINALLY headed to NY for 5 days of relaxation, shopping and fun. I am looooong overdue for a vacation so I am definitely going to shop til I damn near drop! Unfortunately, we still hadn't heard a thing from Angel, so Sara called in some favors with a few officer friends of hers and filed a missing person's report. They promised to give us a call as soon as they heard something.

While I tried to relax and bask in the comfort of this first class seat on the plane, Sara was still racking her brain over the missing Angel.

"So I've been trying to figure out who is sending me the letters. If Angel really IS M.I.A., then who sent this letter? It came to my job just like this; no fingerprints…no nothing."

"Have you looked into the people you sent to jail and got out?" I asked. She said

"Actually I got some buddies looking into it now," she replied.

"So you've told your bosses and the police," I confirmed.

She quickly said "Yes."

I got comfortable in my seat again and said, "Great! So now when I kill a motherfucker, they'll know why. Good looking out Sara."

Sara laughed and said, "Well we can table this for now. We're about to land, which means this vacation is officially about to begin!"

****

I flopped down on the bed, exhausted as hell.

"Damn, Sara," I chuckled. "We've been living it UP in the NYC! We've literally done EVERYTHING and we still have 2 whole days left."

Sara laughed and said "No, not EVERYTHING. We still haven't rode the Staten Island Ferry or had a Coney Island Hot Dog."

I looked at her for a minute and said, "Yeah we can do that.

Then she said she wanted us to do a photoshoot before we left the Big Apple and I suggested we do some erotic poetry somewhere tonight. After we laid out our ideas, Sara said she wanted to talk to me about something serious. I thought her mind had wandered back to the still unheard from Angel, so I listened.

"I've really enjoyed being here with you," she began. "Would you like to make this official?"

I feigned shock. "What you mean? Like be in a relationship?"

She crawled onto the bed next to me and grabbed my hand. "Yes…that's exactly what I mean."

I just gave her a fake smile and told her my decision would be based on what she chooses to do about L.A. and the magazine. Thank God Sara was cool with that answer because this was about to become one more thing that I just did NOT feel like dealing with right now. The sun was beginning to set, so she suggested we take a walk on the beach and try to get in some picture-taking before heading to dinner.

I ran in the bathroom to throw something on right quick and Sara stood in the door, watching me as usual. "You always look so cute Symone."

I smiled and returned the compliment.

Then she rubbed her nipples and said, "Damn Symone…I'mma tear that ass up tonight."

I looked back at her, licked my lips and said, "I bet you are..."

SYMONE

When we returned from New York, Sara had three more letters on her door. They were becoming angrier and much more aggressive. Whoever this person was, they don't like being ignored because now they're threatening her; talking about killing her parents and blowing up her car. So now she's considering going into protective custody and hiring a bodyguard. Angel's sister, Melissa, has requested to have police patrol around her every thirty minutes. This shit is getting very serious, very fast.

I decided now was a great time to check in with Jane. "Girl let me tell you what all I've found out this past week."

"Wait.. first let me tell YOU what's been going on," she interrupted.

"Sam and his lawyer are hiding A LOT from us. The state was granted their final continuance last week and they have until next Friday to present the case or it'll be thrown out."

"Well I sure as hell hope so because I miss my baby," I sighed. "But I found out they think Pablo is a crooked cop; they just don't know to what extent.

This is the reason for all the continuances, because they are literally busting their ass trying to dig up more evidence."

"Hold up....how YOU know?" Jane asked.

"Never mind...it doesn't even matter how you know. It's just awesome that you do. Now, I also found out that Sam's got some heavy shit on the cop. His lawyer told me that if they drop the case, it'll benefit him, but not so much Kim. I say if it benefits one it definitely benefits the other. So if he gets out, so will Kim. The only thing that Sam would have to worry about is being charged with something else."

"I hear they might have to put a new attorney on it because the state's attorney has been getting threats."

Jane went real silent on the phone, as if she was trying to figure out how I had any knowledge of this stuff. Then she said, "I doubt she'll drop; she's too tough. She didn't get where she is today being a softie. They talk about her a lot in the lawyer world."

I was less than impressed.

"Oh...well, I hope it all plays out for the best," I said, rather nonchalantly. "I'm ready for Kim to bring his ass home NOW; it's been like six months already. I mean damn...I could've stayed single for this bullshit. When are you going to see him again?"

"Tomorrow," she replied. "I got to tell him this is their last continuance, as well as everything that Sam's lawyer is saying."

My call waiting beeped; it was Sara. I rolled my eyes and told Jane to call me tomorrow once she got back from seeing Kim. I clicked over and before I could even say hello, her mouth was going a mile a minute, telling me how she'd just received a call from Angel's phone, but when she answered, whoever was on the end simply hung up. She said she called back at least 3 different times, but whoever it was kept hanging up on her. I asked if she heard anything in the background that would give away the caller's identity, but she said there was nothing but utter silence. I told her to the call the police because they should have the means to track the call and she said she did, but the cops told her the person hung up too fast. Then she told me she got yet another letter today; this time the perpetrator put it inside her car. I tried to act as if I cared, asking how the fuck were they able to get inside her car. She was damn near in tears at this point, saying she believed this was an inside job....a ploy to get her to leave her job. I was laughing on the inside, but offered her some encouragement, telling her to do whatever she thought best for her safety.

She did admit that this shit had her shook, but she quickly stated that them bitches in her office got another thing coming if they think she's just going to walk away from one of the biggest cases of her career. I rolled my eyes so hard they almost got stuck in that position. She said she'd decided to hole away in a hotel room for a couple weeks and continue to work her case from there, making sure to invite me over to "play" for a little while. As tempting as that sounded, I had other shit to take care of, so I blew her off, telling her I'd try to come through tomorrow...emphasis on the word TRY.

****

HHD 1

KIM

"Damn K! You've been here for almost for seven months now and not one lady has been here to see you," Ray laughed.

"I don't have a lady," I lied. "I was single when I came here and I'll be single when I leave. I don't want a jailhouse relationship."

"Yeah I hear ya," he agreed. "So I've been hearing your name in these walls. They been sayin' your brother got info on that undercover cop but it don't benefit you bro. I think he's trying to snake you. I got a little clout in here if you got that bread. I can get you some alone time with him."

"How much scratch you talking about?" I asked, very interested.

"Bout $50 for me and $150 for the cop," he replied.

"Once I put you on to my connect, you'll be good from now on. Just don't get him bumped off."

"So what else going around in these walls?" I asked him.

He was all too happy to spill his guts.

"I hear it's a new boss in these streets; her name BB. That's all people know. They don't have any info on her. She got the drug game on lock. This her last shipment she was in and out real quick. She made shit happen. She made a quick 5 million for her and her crew and now they're out the game. I wish I could meet her."

Inside I was screaming "that's my baby!" But all I said was, "Daaaaamn….for real Ray?"

"Word!" he said, getting more and more excited. "I may have to put out the word to get some info on her. Mother fuckers must be too scared to talk about her or something."

"Damn maybe she got mob connections," I suggested. "You know how ruthless they are. They'll off your whole family."

"Yeah that's true," he nodded. "But I still want to know who she is though. I wanna get my people and me on. Someone is talking hard in these streets. How else would they know she made 5 million in the game and now she out?"

"Just find the one that's talking and they'll keep talking for little or nothing."

"Word," Ray replied. "So what they saying about your case KB?"

I shook my head. "They saying this lawyer on some ol' bullshit with all these unnecessary continuances. I think it's some real shit going wrong with this case and I hope it all falls apart cause I'm going to sue the shit outta them. That's all I know so far though." I sighed long and hard.

"I hope my lawyer got some more info for me today cause a nigga like me wanna take a long hot bath. May sound gay but it's true," I laughed. "I want to put on some real clothes and use some real lotion and soap. I want to do some 'real nigga shit': eat some pussy, smack some ass or something."

Ray laughed. "I feel you dawg! I miss all that shit too. I DO know a few female officers in here that can make that happen for you though."

I quickly refused. "Nawl dawg. I'm good. But when you find out that info on ol' girl though, let me know."

"I just thought about a man that has a big crew that can get off her kind of weight," he said. "I'll ask and see if he can set something up."

"Yeah set that meeting up with my bro asap," I said.

"I gotcha bro."

"Oh one last thing," I said. "I need to meet the man in here. I'll make it worth your while."

He didn't even have to think about it.

"Damn...I'm real low on food so that'll work. I'll have you meet him when he come on shift in the morning."

After Ray walked off to holla at some other dudes, my mind immediately went into overdrive. *My baby is out here making some hardcore moves; got people sniffing trying to find out who she is.* I chuckled to myself. *So she a boss now, huh? I'mma have to tell her to fall back a little cause bitches in here nosy and the streets is starting to talk. I know one damn thing....Sam better start telling me some good shit when I see him or it's going to be some problems. Real talk.*

✳✳✳✳✳✳✳✳✳✳✳✳✳✳✳✳✳✳✳✳✳✳✳✳✳

The next morning, the duty guard came by my cell. "You have a visitor."

I was shocked when I walked into the meeting room; Ray actually came through.

"K! What up bro?" Sam said, standing up.

"What's good man?" We dapped and hugged each other, then I got right down to business.

"So what's really going on with this Pablo character? What you got on him?"

He immediately got nervous. "Man K...if I give up what I have on him, I'll never get out."

I got angry. "What you mean? Just say the shit! This a clean room. I paid good money for this meeting. I been in here for 7 ½ months and I need to know some shit! Is he crooked or not?"

He just sat there....biting his lips and shaking his leg. He was starting to piss me the hell. Finally he said, "Yeah...but not how y'all think."

He went dead silent again, so I said, "Ok...? Then how? Look bro...I ain't gonna put you in a situation where you'll end up having to stay here. I just need to know what's going on. Maybe our lawyers can put they heads together and get us the fuck up outta here. I need some pussy bro! I'm tired of looking at niggas…for real. And I know you miss your lady."

He smiled and licked his lips. "Hell yeah I miss that phat ass. Shit…I miss sleeping in my own damn bed most of all."

I grabbed his shoulders and shook him. "So spill the beans fool!"

He sighed.

"A'ight check this out…ol' boy is stealing money off the drug dealers when they raid the houses and trap spots. At first, I didn't know he was a cop until it was too late. He came in like he was a customer in my store. I was cleaning his money with our money; that's how I got caught up in this shit. I know damn well he ain't turning that money over. Ain't nothin' bout him clean. He be having money stuffed in his vest and in his underwear and shit. Undercovers don't do that shit…"

He took a breath for air and continued..

"… At first, I put it in an account overseas for him, but I think he moved it. I got my lawyer looking into it. All the paperwork is at the office."

"I know," I replied.

"Symone found it and gave it to her sister. We've been trying to figure out when and where you've been hiding the money and why you were hiding it. Now I see. I thought you were hanging me out to dry. So the money overseas is in HIS name then?" He said

"No…that's the catch," Sam shook his head.

"It's in his WIFE'S name in one of the accounts, and in both of their names in the other. Thing is though, she don't work and never have. So where the hell would she get THAT type of money?"

He scooted up in his chair and leaned all the way across the table. "This mofo even got dirty police money from a human trafficking sting that he stole and said the people ran off with it. I never sent it over there though; I kept it for my safety in case he tried to trap me, like now. I just want to know that I won't go down too. I know I could've BEEN got our case thrown out but I was seriously scared shitless."

I dapped him up again as I stood up to leave.

"Well let's work together to get out. I miss the outside world."

****

HHD 1

SYMONE

"Marvin is this line clear?"

"You good BB," he confirmed.

"Somebody in your crew talking real good,"

I said. "And this is coming from the jail."

He was shocked. "Damn really? I bet I know who it is."

"But what I need to know is who he's getting his info from," I replied.

"It's only me and one other person who know who you are and all he know is you are the connect."

"That's all the streets know," I said. "But they're looking for more info now. I don't want to be known."

He quickly said, "I'll take care of it. He'll be dealt with, because one thing you don't do in this game is talk. If he discussing you then he discussing me. That brings police."

"Say no more," I said. "Thanks."

****

HHD 1

KIM

As I was headed back to my cell a couple of days later, Ray suddenly came speed-walking towards me. I've never seen such a midnight black dude look so pale. This can't be good.

"K, I put out the word to get the info on the boss but shit, I guess my man was digging too hard. Him and his family got whacked....ALL of 'em. They ain't have to do him like that."

"Oh shit...." I think I went pale at that moment too. "What happened?"

Ray's eyes began to pool with tears. "They cut the man's tongue out and stuffed a rat in his mouth. Then they chopped his dick off, put it next to him and wrote 'snitch' on his chest. They put three holes in his wife's head and took his dad out in the woods and slit his throat."

He shook his head sadly as he continued. "The whole hood fucked up; talking about going to war. I told them shit like that is the mob. Leave that shit alone cause they'll never know who done that. He must've been talking to a lot of people in the streets." If Ray's head hung any lower, his nose would've been touching his shoestrings. "K I know he fucked up, but they didn't have to do him and his peoples like that. That was my cousin yo... I guess they wanted to send a message."

My heart was racing. "Damn bro... I'm so sorry this happened. Money will be on your books by tomorrow. And thank you again for hooking me up with my bro." We dapped and hugged before Ray walked off, head still dragging the ground.

My blood went cold. *Has my baby really become THIS ruthless? I need to get outta here fast; they're turning her into a cold-hearted monster. I need to get her out and soften her back up to the Sy I know and love.*

****

HHD 1

SYMONE

I'm sending my mom, Momma B and Kesh off to NAPA Valley for a nice little mini vaycay. They leave tomorrow right after the grand opening and I'm glad about it because they need to get away for a minute, especially Kesh. I went to Sara's last night and all she kept talking about was Angel and those damn letters. I hated to be mean, but I cut that visit REAL short and went and kicked it with Sherry and Jasmine at The Cheesecake Factory. Those two are hilarious and kept me in tears laughing the entire night; I really needed that.

Later that evening, I went over to AJ's house to check out his Sheem'a collection. I was in heaven!

He gave me some bomb ass mini dresses and accessories plus a dope pair Jimmy Choo stilettos.

I've been on a hardcore house-hunting grind lately. I want to make sure everything is already settled by the time my baby gets out. I've seen three already: one in Orland, one in Matteson and one in Tinley Park, and I'm going to see one in Park Forest tomorrow. I really like the one in Matteson. It's a five br/4.5 ba with a full basement, eat-in kitchen, den and a full closed in backyard with a deck and an in-ground swimming pool. It was absolutely beautiful, and at only $220,000, it's also rather easy on the pockets. If this one in Park Forest doesn't top that one in Matteson by leaps and bounds, then Matteson is the clear winner. And, once K gets out, that beautiful house will finally be a home. *I'm sick of all this grimy ass shit I've had to resort to just to hold him down. I just want my regular life back...with my man, our new home and the family we're working to build. This right here....ain't me, and I'm not sure how much more of this I can handle on my own.*

Jane texted me to let me know she had more letters from K for me. I told her I'd be over tomorrow to pick them up.

****

I went to see Sara the next day. She was looking all sad like a caged animal. I know she wants to get out of here, but every two or three days she gets a letter and now her parents have started getting them. The only people she could think of that were capable of something like this is the mob or drug cartel people. She does remember sending away a guy high up in the drug cartel two years ago, but she was confused why he'd wait til now to strike back, so she said she went to see him yesterday. He laughed in her face and claimed not to know what the hell she was talking about. He just said "karma is a bitch" and dismissed her. She said she wanted to rip his fucking head off his neck. She said she wished she could monitor his calls and mail but she didn't have enough evidence against him. So she's at a complete loss now, because whoever is doing this is so good at it, they're leaving no prints or anything on the letters. One thing she's very adamant about though is that everyone makes a mistake eventually.

I asked her had she heard anything else from Angel's phone and she said unfortunately no but her sister's husband was able to call in a favor and had the local news do a missing person's report, and she made it clear that she's not leaving til her sister is found....alive. At that moment, I cut the conversation short, using the Bears game I was about to go to as my excuse to break out.

As scared as she is for her life, it didn't stop her nasty ass from getting fresh with me. "Damn...I was hoping I could bury my face in that tonight."

I looked over my shoulder as I walked out the door and said, "Maybe I'll stop back over here tonight....if I feel like it."

****

Me: "Hey boo."

Mel: "Don't hey boo me, I haven't hit that in like 2 months."

Me: "I know that's one of the reasons I'm calling you."

Mel: "What's the other reason?"

Me: "I need a favor."

Mel: "I like doing favors for you. You pay good and in many ways."

Me: "I want to give you an advance on this one."

Mel: "Come see me tonight around 8 at my house."

Me: "See ya then."

HHD 1

I made it to the condo before her; about five minutes later she rang the bell. I had a really nice movie night planned for us but first we needed to discuss major business. I explained to her that I needed her to catch that officer's wife at the salon, the store, the park; wherever the hell she goes during the day with their baby, and give her a letter but don't say who it's from. The letter needs to let her know that her husband is keeping secrets from her; that he has her name tangled up in some dirty overseas money; and when he goes down, she's going down too. I told her to make sure she didn't touch the letter with her bare hands because we didn't want her running it for prints. I know I shouldn't care, but the only way to truly hurt him is to drive his family away. Then once they're gone, I'll really hit him where it hurt."

"Daaaaamn," Mel said, shaking her head. "Bitch remind me to never cross you and yours. Where have you been hiding this evil side?"

"I ain't evil," I smiled. "I just go all out for mines."

HHD 1

Marvin was waiting for me at 'the spot' when I got there.

"Soooooo…" I said, strolling in with a huge grin on my face. "How have you been treating my prisoner Marvin?"

He laughed and said, "She good. She ask a lot of questions. I'm sure she's tired of that dungeon." I told him

"She'll be set free in due time," I said. "Nobody's touched her right?"

"Nope," Marvin promised. "She just sits there watching TV and sleeping all day. She whines and cries a lot, but that's about it."

"Here go feed her and snap a picture," I said handing him the phone. "And make sure you wipe the phone down. I'll pay you big when it's done."

"BB why every time you come here you got on gloves?" he asked.

"I like my freedom," I smirked.

He laughed. "Nuff said. You need me to run to the other trap and grab the cash we almost done with?"

"No I want it all at once."

"Cool. Give me four more weeks then. I got a few people coming from the D to grab some stuff."

"Marv are you going to miss the game when it's done?" I asked him.

"Actually, I was going to ask you can you hook me up with the connect after this," he replied. "I could damn sure use my own money. I'm trying to get to boss status."

"One favor deserves another....I'll make it happen," I promised.

"Thank you Sis. I'll owe you."

"Nawl you cool my dude." I started heading towards to the door. "A'ight I'm out; call me when you through."

"I'm all over it. I ain't failed you yet. Top notch secret."

****

As soon as I left 'the spot' I met Mel at her office.

"Ok what you got for me?" I asked anxiously.

HHD 1

"Well, I met her at the park with little Sean and I sat next to her as if I were a parent or nanny," Mel began relaying the story.

"She started talking and asking me do I have any children and stuff like that. I told her no; I was there to see her. So now she's trying to figure out who I am. I had on some dark shades and a scarf wrapped like Mary J Blige in the "Not Gon' Cry' video. I wore black lipstick and some forearm length gloves. Girl I was fierce!" she snapped her fingers and we both laughed.

"So I got straight to business; asked her if she knew her husband had dirty money overseas in her name. She was shocked; turned white as a fucking ghost. I told her if we go off these particular records, you have over $150,000 in your account and $250,000 in the joint account. I was like where the fuck did you two get this kind of money from a cop salary? She said she didn't know but she was sure going to find out and took the papers.

By this point, she's beet damn red. She did ask me how I knew all this. I told her I know people who know people." We both laughed again.

HHD 1

"So I reiterated to her that her husband is a dirty cop and once everything comes out about him he'll lose his job and more than likely his pension too, so if I was you, I would take every single drop of that money and leave now; otherwise the government is going to freeze it and then your family will have nothing. She was crying and asking me who else knows about this. I told her enough people obviously that I found out and now you know. I assured that in a week's time, the right people will know so this is her one and only heads-up. I told her I was genuinely concerned about her and her kids' well-being and the last thing I wanted was for them to be effected by her husband's wrong doing. As I walked away I told her to enjoy her new found riches."

"Yeeeeesssss!" I girly squealed.

"Great job Mel! You laid that shit just right! Now let's just sit back and see how 'nicely' this ends up..."

ABOUT THE AUTHOR

Sheem'a was born in raised in Chicago, IL. where she enjoys spending time with her family and friends. She has a great passion for writing and does it quite often.

She put writing on hold to enjoy the honeymoon phase of her marriage but has now resumed with renewed vigor.

She is the mother of 5 children; 3 biological and 2 stepchildren. She has even encouraged her children to start their own book series.

Sheem'a has started her own lipstick called Flawlezz Puckerz...

"Where every woman can go from ordinary to extraordinary..." Sheem'a

HHD 1

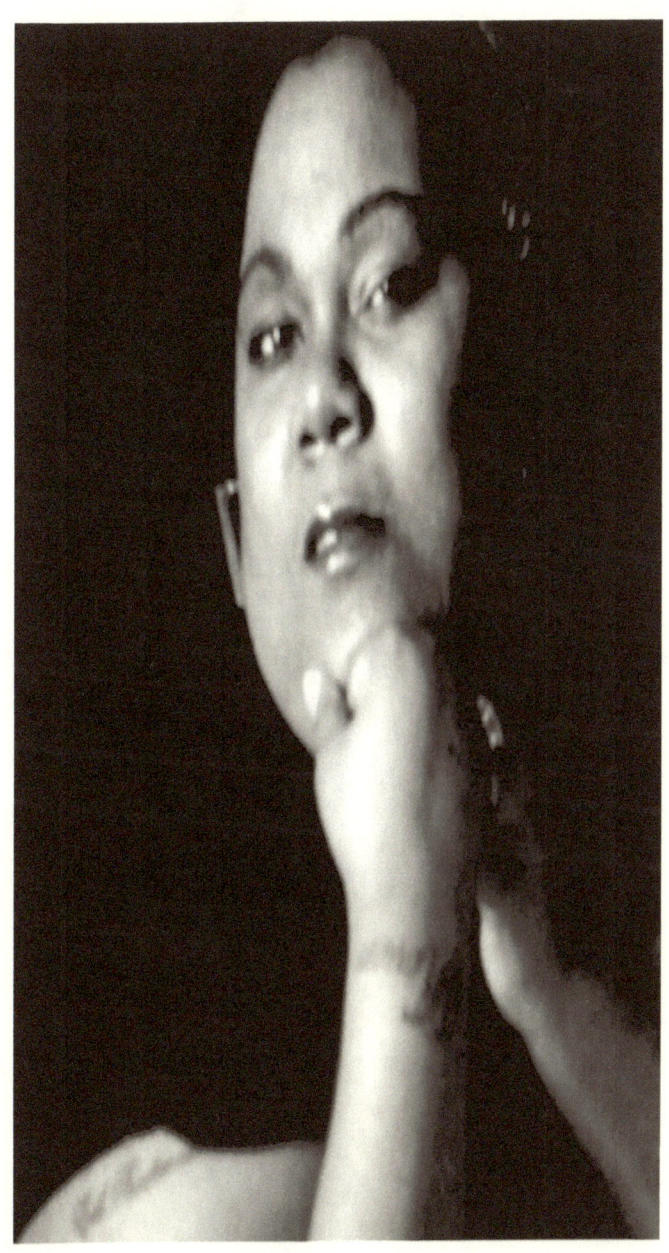

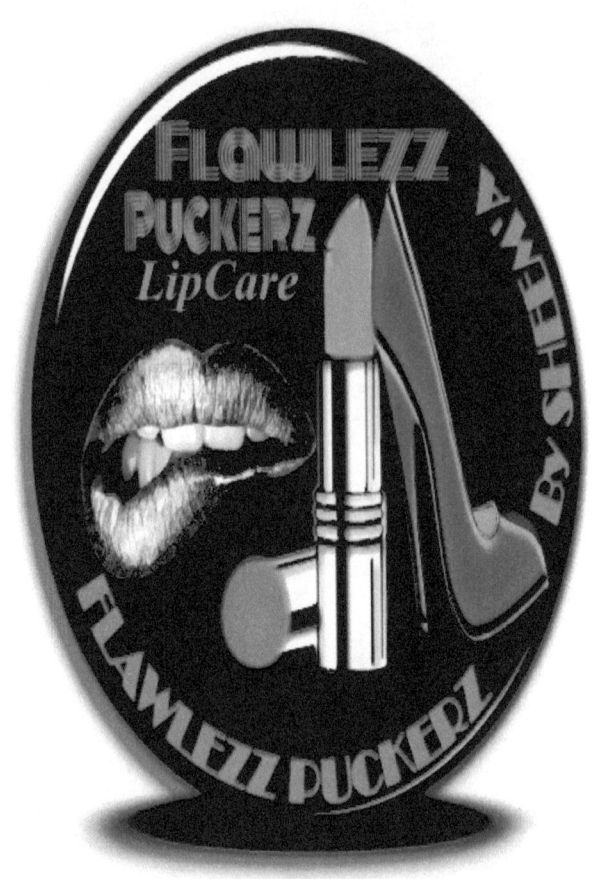

flawlezzpuckerz.wix.com/flawlezz-puckerz

www.ingramcontent.com/pod-product-compliance
Lightning Source LLC
Chambersburg PA
CBHW020410150626
46554CB00012B/578